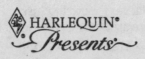

Welcome to the September 2008 collection of
Harlequin Presents!

This month, be sure to read favorite author
Penny Jordan's *Virgin for the Billionaire's Taking*,
in which virginal Keira is whisked off to the exotic
world of handsome Jay! Michelle Reid brings you a
fabulous tale of a ruthless Italian's convenient bride
in *The De Santis Marriage*, while Carol Marinelli's
gorgeous tycoon wants revenge on innocent Caitlyn
in *Italian Boss, Ruthless Revenge*. And don't miss
the final story in Carole Mortimer's brilliant trilogy
THE SICILIANS, *The Sicilian's Innocent Mistress!*
Abby Green brings you the society wedding of
the year in *The Kouros Marriage Revenge*, and in
Chantelle Shaw's *At The Sheikh's Bidding*, Erin's life
is changed forever when she discovers her adopted
son is heir to a desert kingdom!

Also this month, new author Heidi Rice delivers a
sizzling, sexy boss in *The Tycoon's Very Personal
Assistant*, and in Ally Blake's *The Magnate's Indecent
Proposal*, an ordinary girl is faced with a millionaire
who's way out of her league. Enjoy!

We'd love to hear what you think about Harlequin
Presents. E-mail us at Presents@hmb.co.uk or join
in the discussions at www.iheartpresents.com and
www.sensationalromance.blogspot.com, where
you'll also find more information about books and
authors!

Private jets. Luxury cars. Exclusive five-star hotels.
Designer outfits for every occasion and an
entourage of staff to see to your every whim....

In this brand-new collection, ordinary women
step into the world of the super-rich and are

He'll have her, but at what price?

Available only from Harlequin Presents®.

Ally Blake

THE MAGNATE'S INDECENT PROPOSAL

TAKEN BY THE
MILLIONAIRE

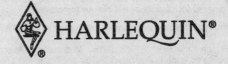

HARLEQUIN®

TORONTO • NEW YORK • LONDON
AMSTERDAM • PARIS • SYDNEY • HAMBURG
STOCKHOLM • ATHENS • TOKYO • MILAN • MADRID
PRAGUE • WARSAW • BUDAPEST • AUCKLAND

If you purchased this book without a cover you should be aware that this book is stolen property. It was reported as "unsold and destroyed" to the publisher, and neither the author nor the publisher has received any payment for this "stripped book."

ISBN-13: 978-0-373-12762-7
ISBN-10:   0-373-12762-6

THE MAGNATE'S INDECENT PROPOSAL

First North American Publication 2008.

Copyright © 2008 by Ally Blake.

All rights reserved. Except for use in any review, the reproduction or utilization of this work in whole or in part in any form by any electronic, mechanical or other means, now known or hereafter invented, including xerography, photocopying and recording, or in any information storage or retrieval system, is forbidden without the written permission of the publisher, Harlequin Enterprises Limited, 225 Duncan Mill Road, Don Mills, Ontario, Canada M3B 3K9.

This is a work of fiction. Names, characters, places and incidents are either the product of the author's imagination or are used fictitiously, and any resemblance to actual persons, living or dead, business establishments, events or locales is entirely coincidental.

This edition published by arrangement with Harlequin Books S.A.

® and TM are trademarks of the publisher. Trademarks indicated with ® are registered in the United States Patent and Trademark Office, the Canadian Trade Marks Office and in other countries.

www.eHarlequin.com

Printed in U.S.A.

All about the author...
Ally Blake

When **ALLY BLAKE** was a little girl, she made a
wish that when she turned twenty-six she would
marry an Italian two years older than herself.
After it actually came true, she realized she was
on to something with these wish things. So,
next she wished that she could make a living
spending her days in her pajamas, eating M&M's
and drinking scads of coffee while using her
formative experiences of wallowing in teenage
crushes and romantic movies to create love
stories of her own. The fact that she is now able
to spend her spare time searching the Internet
for pictures of handsome guys for research
purposes is merely a bonus! Come along and
visit her Web site at www.allyblake.com.

To my editor, Bryony Green.

Thank you for discovering me, indulging me with unexpected opportunities and knowing just how to draw the best writing out of me. None of this would have been possible without you.

CHAPTER ONE

CHELSEA flicked a stray streak of wet mud off the nose of the beagle motif on her old umbrella as she ducked under the silver and black striped awning of Amelie's, a newly opened Melbourne restaurant a stone's throw from the Yarra River at South Bank.

She peered through the floor-to-ceiling windows to see the place was peppered with bright and shiny types decked out in designer gear. While the chocolate-brown knee-length skirt she'd found in the back of her closet sat at a slightly askew angle to hide a fresh doggie shampoo stain.

'In a couple of hours I'll be out of these high-heeled boots and back into sneakers,' she said aloud. 'While you'll all have bunions before you're forty.'

As some kind of perverse justice, her boots teetered beneath her as she twirled out of the way of a rushing pair of suits barging out of the restaurant barking into their mobile phones rather than looking out for stray women on the pavement.

Not wanting to push her luck, she slipped inside the glass doors and patted the criss-cross of bobby pins holding back her too-long fringe to make sure they were still in place and not dangling from the end of her hair like some odd mobile.

'Do you have a reservation?' the skinny, bald *maître d'* in head-to-toe black asked.

'I'm Chelsea London,' she said, leaning back slightly to make sure he wouldn't get a waft of the mothball scent of her recently de-cupboarded fancy clothes. 'Meeting Kensington Hurley. She's always madly early. I'd be happy to sneak through and find her myself—'

'Not necessary.' He gave her a cool smile.

Phoney schmuck, she thought as she gave him a weak smile in return.

He ran a bony finger down the pale pink diary page and nodded. Then said, 'Your phone, please.'

'Excuse me, my what?' said Chelsea.

'Your…mobile…phone,' he repeated, more slowly this time. 'They are a nuisance to other customers thus we don't allow them in the restaurant. You would have been told at the time of reservation.'

'My sister chose this place,' she explained through gritted teeth.

'Nevertheless, you need to check it into the cloakroom.'

She bit her lip while she made up her mind about what to do. Her whole life was in her phone. Her address book, her appointments calendar, her grocery list, her emails, the profit and loss statements to take to the bank later that morning now that she'd finally made an appointment with a loan officer to see about expanding Pride & Groom, her pet-grooming business, from one salon to three. He might as well have asked for her future firstborn child for all it meant to her.

She sank her hand into her oversized handbag and held it tight as she asked, 'What if I don't have a phone?'

He kept his hand outstretched, palm up.

'Okay, fine,' she said, doing a quick, obsessive-compulsive

message check before handing it over. 'But couldn't you just ask everyone to turn their phone to silent? And confiscate those who don't comply?'

'This isn't high school, Ms London. We believe mobile phones are antisocial. And haven't you come here today to be social?'

High school is for ever, she thought. *Those in new uniforms compared with those in hand-me-downs, all living out the failures or successes of their parents like some great evolutionary joke.*

She kept her theory to herself and instead muttered, 'I came here today because my sister has the kind of big brown cow eyes you can't say no to.'

He gave her a pink ticket with a smudged black number written upon it in return, then she pressed on into the restaurant.

Weaving her way through the tightly packed tables past a plethora of 'new school uniform' types with money and time and an apparent desire to be social on a Tuesday morning, she made a determined beeline for Kensey's curly brown 'do. Thus she didn't notice a gentleman prepare to slide back his chair until it was too late.

She put on the brakes but her inexperience in her high-heeled boots meant she lost her grip upon the swanky silk carpet. Her momentum pitched her forward and everything from that point on seemed to happen in slow motion.

The man turned, alerted by either the whoosh of air she displaced before her, or perhaps the frantic oath she'd emitted a second before that. As she fell she found herself amidst one of those time-stood-still-while-my-life-flashed-before-my-eyes moments as she made eye contact with her attacker, whose features burned onto her brain one after the other.

A toothpick between perfect white front teeth. Smooth dark

hair so neat it looked as if it had been cut that morning. A jaw line so defined it made a girl want to reach out and run the back of her finger along it. Dark glinting eyes the colour of the Pacific just before dusk.

Even that tremendous collection of visual stimuli wasn't enough to stop the laws of physics. Chelsea had no choice but to reach out and grab him by two handfuls of his suit jacket to stop herself from going completely head over heels.

He instinctively slid both arms around her middle, slowing her momentum until she came to a complete stop. Upright, or almost, considering her legs were twisted, she clung. Bodily against him. Her breasts pressed into his chest. Her stomach hard against the zipper of his trousers. Her shaky right knee clamped snug between both of his. She knew enough about the shape of him that in some cultures they'd be considered be-trothed.

She curled her fingers gently beneath a lapel or two. His suit felt *really* nice. Expensive. The fabric was soft and warm. And it smelled so good. Like falling leaves and crisp fresh air. At least she assumed it was the suit. Maybe it was just him.

When time finally caught up with her, the surrounds of the restaurant swarmed in. Clinking cutlery. Tinkling laughter. Steam from the kitchen. The feel of his long thin wallet beneath her knuckles and next to his heart. And the intermingling whisper of the pair of them breathing heavily.

'Are you okay?' he asked. His voice was husky. Deep. It rumbled through her hands and into her chest until it found a home deep within her stomach. She gave into the need to lick suddenly bone-dry lips.

'Hey,' he rumbled again, and tucked a finger beneath her chin, lifting her gaze to his face as he repeated, 'Are you okay?'

His skin was unblemished and evenly tanned, his eyes so

blue it hurt, and he truly smelled beautiful, like the rainy autumn day she'd left outside. All that glowing, carefree perfection made him as tempting as the yummiest forbidden fruit. But this gal had already eaten away her lip-gloss, her clothes were a decade old, and she smelled like wet dog and mothballs. Thus forbidden fruit would never be hers to have.

She slowly let her grip abate.

'I'm fine,' Chelsea said. 'Dandy, in fact. Embarrassed, but there seems to be no permanent damage to the patch of carpet my boots did their best to take on. It could have been worse.'

'True,' he said. 'If there'd been a dessert cart in the vicinity we would very quickly have become a scene out of a Pink Panther film.'

Her cheeks twitched in amusement. 'Can't you imagine a barrage of chocolate cream pies flying through the air and landing on *that* table of coiffed princesses until they are dripping in pearls *and* chocolate sauce?'

The man's eyes darted sideways to the table of women who had been eyeing Chelsea as she had walked in. And he said, 'It would certainly have added a dash of sunshine to such a drab morning.'

As he smiled at her some more, his eyes now twinkling, his toothpick twirling as though behind his teeth his tongue was hard at work, Chelsea's stomach felt unnaturally hollow. And she didn't think it had all that much to do with hunger for food.

She smiled back, all lips, no teeth, and then proceeded to disentangle herself as elegantly as she could manage. But once she'd let go she discovered she'd scrunched up his lovely suit lapels something awful. She spent a good ten seconds flattening them out, running her hands along the soft wool, which did little to hide the hard body beneath.

'Though I'm not sure I could handle any more sunshine

than I have right now,' he said, his voice ever deeper, and so close she could feel the air of every word brush against her fast-warming cheek.

She bit. 'And why's that?'

'I've never before had a woman fall for me quite so quickly. Usually I count on an introduction and a little flirtation before the sunshine part.'

She glanced up into his eyes again. Deep. Absorbing. Blue as the heavens. He was pure charm. And she had the distinct feeling he knew it. Which meant he also knew she was no longer hanging onto him for balance.

She stopped her fussing and said, 'One little hint? Next time you're looking to land yourself a girl, don't bother with the chair. Props are for amateurs.'

His playful smile faded until it was no more than a glimmer in his eyes. He breathed in through his nose, she felt it in the swell of his chest, and then realised that to all intents and purposes she was still feeling the guy up. She gave his lapels one last tug, then said, 'Now nobody will know I was ever here.'

He removed the toothpick and with his deep voice so low only a person a mere breath away would be able to hear him he said, 'I'll know.'

His words slid through her, hot, liquid, and unimpeded by any kind of sense or self-defence. In a stab of unadulterated desire it occurred to her that if she slanted her head an inch, two at the most, she could find out if his smiling lips tasted anywhere near as good as they looked.

She took an abrupt step back and bumped his table hard enough his full latte glass rocked mercilessly and sloshed a gulp or two over the edge. Mr Suit and Tie leapt for the glass and caught it just before it tilted all the way over.

Free of his autumnal scent, his magnetic gaze, and the

pleasure of luxurious wool, Chelsea slid out of his gravita-tional pull. 'That's my cue to leave before I accidentally set you on fire.'

'No, wait,' he said, putting the glass back on the table, and patting down the polished wood with a napkin.

But she hitched her handbag higher onto her shoulder, and then eased around him and hurried to join her sister on the other side of the restaurant.

Kensey stood, kissed her cheek. 'Tell me you got his phone number,' were the first words out of her mouth.

Chelsea dumped her bag beneath the table, sat, then threw her hands over her face, cooling her hot cheeks with her freez-ing palms. 'And when was I meant to have done that in between throwing myself in his arms and knocking over his drink?'

'What's your number, honey?' Kensey said. 'You can find time between anything for four such important words. Espe-cially for such a specimen as that one.'

Chelsea came out from behind her hands to glare at her sister. 'And this from a married woman.'

'You're comparing Greg to *that*?'

Chelsea glared some more. 'Don't you dare intimate Greg isn't the best thing that ever happened to you.'

Greg with his thinning hair and thickening middle wasn't Chelsea's type, but every time she saw the two of them together it only reminded her she shouldn't be so picky. Kensey and Greg were mad for one another while she didn't have any man who'd take her hand as they walked down the street, whose shoulder she could lean on at the movies, to hold her when she fell asleep.

'How do you think a girl gets herself married these days?' Kensey asked. 'It takes putting herself on the shop shelf to begin with.'

'I like dating,' Chelsea said. 'Especially men with muscles and dark eyes and all their teeth. I'm *on* the shelf.'

'Right. With a big Do Not Feed the Animal sign slung around your neck. One sideways glance at another woman, one bounced cheque, one hint he might have feet of clay and you bite the hand that fondles you. Whereas that creature over there is so-o-o on the shelf fluorescent lights aim towards him wherever he goes.'

Chelsea scoffed, then twisted to sling her cropped jacket over the back of her chair and spared a glance back through the restaurant to the man in question. He was standing talking to another guy in a suit. One hand was pushing his jacket back as he searched his trouser pocket, revealing an expanse of neat white business shirt stretched just tight enough across a broad chest to make it difficult to look away.

Like the first wisp of smoke heralding a coming fire, a thread of longing curled through her stomach. Her fingernails dug patterns into her palms as she imagined tearing open that flawless expensive starched white shirt until the buttons popped off.

She blinked hard at the ferocity of her reaction. It wasn't as though she didn't come in contact with any number of good-looking men every day of her life. Her job gave her a veritable platter to choose from. Nice men, responsible men, men who loved dogs, men who were well and truly within her comfort zone.

In the past couple of months there had been an Alsatian owner who was also a plumber. Cute. Brawny. He'd unblocked her pipes in the shop but not in any other way worth mentioning. She'd let him go when he'd let on he loved betting on the greyhounds. Then there'd been the Bijon Frise owner, a single dad who only had the dog as he'd inherited it in his divorce along with the kids every second weekend. She'd let him go when he'd cried watching a long-distance phone ad. And the consultant with the matching set of fox terriers called Mitsy and Bitsy. She'd turned him down after one dinner for obvious reasons.

But comparing those dating experiences with three minutes spent looking into a pair of Pacific blue eyes made her wonder briefly if responsibility, sense, and comfort were all they were cracked up to be. Mr Suit and Tie and Flirty Look in the Eye made her hanker for fire, flash, flare, electricity, excitement, heat, danger, no care for the consequences…

Right then a dark, glossy brunette in a tight black skirt suit and heels so high Chelsea felt dizzy just looking at them walked by, landed a flat hand upon Mr Suit and Tie's chest and leaned in to whisper something in his ear. Mr Suit and Tie laughed, said something that made the brunette flutter a hand across her face before sauntering away swinging her hips like a pro. He paid attention for a few moments, and then pulled a flat black wallet from the inner pocket of his jacket before letting it swing back into place.

Chelsea came to as if fairy dust had suddenly cleared from before her eyes. She turned back to Kensey, who was watching her with a knowing smile on her face.

'He's a man. He's moved onto the next sure thing,' Chelsea insisted with a scowl. 'Big surprise there.'

'Fine,' Kensey said with a dramatic sigh. 'So how's work?'

'Great. Fun. Hard. Wouldn't trade it for anything. The kids?'

'Great. Fun. Hard. Wouldn't trade 'em for anything. So are you coming to the Yarra Valley with us this weekend? It's Lucy's birthday, remember.'

'Of course. Wouldn't miss it for the world.'

'You know you don't have to come alone. If you ever wanted to bring someone…'

'How about I bring Phyllis? She loves country air,' Chelsea said, referring to her longest-serving employee, a six-foot-tall woman with short grey hair and a booming voice who terrified the bejeezers out of Kensey.

'I meant a man.'

'If it's that important to you I'll see if I can pick one up on the road along the way. Tell Greg he'll have the darts partner he's always wanted, though I can't promise the guy will have bathed in some time.'

Kensey's gaze slid down to the tabletop where Chelsea was wringing her hands. 'Relax. Please. This is meant to be a celebration breakfast.'

'I haven't got the loan yet.'

'You will. Pride & Groom is just the kind of thing banks want to get their claws into.'

'You've been working on that line for days, haven't you?'

'The whole month,' Kensey said. 'But I'm serious. You own your shop outright. You've been on the telly. You're a woman. You are quite simply dripping in reasons for them to invest in you.'

Chelsea had a sudden image of the brunette in the black suit *dripping* in chocolate-cream pie, which made her smile. But when it rather quickly morphed into a certain dark-haired man *sans* suit and tie dripping in chocolate sauce her mouth began to water.

He's a prince of the 'new school uniform' set, she yelled inside her head. *You're the leftovers of a hand-me-down youth. And never the twain shall successfully mate.*

Along those lines Chelsea reminded her sister, 'You know how much trouble Dad got himself into over the years, borrowing against each new get-rich-quick scheme while the bastards just let him. Keeping Pride & Groom as a one-off, boutique, secure investment wouldn't be a silly idea.'

And it would remain all hers. Something nobody could take away from her. Even though she had to turn away more clients every time she appeared on TV, or had her salon highlighted in a magazine, making her think Pride & Groom could be really beyond-her-wildest-dreams successful. The problem with that was she'd learnt young just how crushing wild dreams could be if they didn't come true.

'Honey,' Kensey said, 'you want to update this outfit of yours to something of this century, you're gonna need more money. You wanna find yourself with more opportunities to go chest to chest with the likes of Hunka Hunka Burning Love over there, you're gonna need more money. If they offer the loan, take it.'

Chelsea leaned forward and whispered conspiratorially, 'Why? You think he's a male escort? What is the going rate these days?'

Kensey's eyes narrowed. 'No idea. But I do know you're a fool not to have given him your phone number. Or at least an accidental grope of that fantastic backside.'

Chelsea leaned back and picked up the menu. 'Maybe next time,' she said, then did her best to keep her eyes in her head when she caught a load of the prices. Nearly thirty dollars for a poached egg on toast? Seriously. What *did* these people have to promise the gods to be able to afford to eat like this on a daily basis?

'He watched you walk the whole way over here, you know,' Kensey said.

Rather than answer, Chelsea stole Kensey's iced water and took a sip.

'Top to bottom,' Kensey said, 'with a nice lingering moment spent on your behind.'

'He was probably trying to see where I was hiding it. If the bank was giving away curvier curves and charging interest then I'd be first in line.'

Boobs that could fill a bra without padding, hips that swung as she walked without the chance of pulling a muscle, the kind of figure that would garner the attention of a man like Mr Suit and Tie without having to literally throw herself at him. Though what she'd do with the likes of such an alien creature if she ever caught him, she had no idea.

'Truthfully, he was probably making sure I didn't knock over any other poor unsuspecting patrons,' she said. 'Most men like to think themselves knights in shining armour.'

'Maybe that one really is.'

'Well, then, he's the last thing I need. I rescued myself a long time ago.'

'Then how about a bit of rough and tumble? How long has it been since you indulged in a scintillating affair? No plans. No future. No "what kind of dog does he own and what does it mean in terms of his level of responsibleness?" but just hot, sweaty nakedness—'

'Okay, I get it!'

Kensey motioned over Chelsea's shoulder. Chelsea glanced back to find the gentleman making his way towards the front door looking unfrazzled by a single thing in his perfect world, and completely untouched by the eyes of a dozen women burning into his back. He really was so beautiful, so tempting, it physically hurt. But if he took responsibility for another creature more animated than a pet rock, she'd be very much surprised.

'One night,' Kensey said. 'With that. Satisfaction guaranteed.'

Chelsea gave into a few last moments gazing over gorgeous tailoring, dark neat hair, broad shoulders and lithe movement born of pure male confidence before turning back to her sister with a blank face.

'I told you I didn't even get a name. And I don't think sky-writing "Trying to track down tall dark handsome man in suit" over the city is going to help. Hot, sweaty nakedness will simply have to wait.'

Kensey raised both eyebrows, sucked in her cheeks and picked up her menu and Chelsea hoped that would be the end of it. Until her sister said, 'We can switch seats so you can make final eyes at him, if you'd like.'

'I'm fine. Thanks anyway.'

Besides, the mirrored wall behind Kensey showed him patting his Suit and Tie friend on the back as together they weaved through the tightly cramped tables and headed back to Stock Market Land or wherever it was they stored such glorious, un-touchable, never-had-to-work-up-a-sweat-to-get-everything-they-ever-wanted creatures once they'd drifted happily through high school and beyond.

Chelsea harnessed her concentration, whipped it back into line and focussed fully on her sister. 'Now, enough about me and my behind—what's been happening in your world?'

CHAPTER TWO

'YOUR tickets, sir?'

Damien reached into his jacket pocket and pulled out the pink stub for his phone and the grey one for his coat. He handed them over to the skinny blonde *femme fatale* who'd taken over from the snappish guy as *maître d'*.

Ticket stub in hand, she bent to the locked boxes at the bottom of the closet, showcasing the edge of a black lace G-string atop her tight denim.

'Nice,' Caleb said from behind him.

'All yours,' Damien murmured back.

'Sure she's no Bonnie...'

'I thought we'd agreed that name was banned for the meantime.'

'You agreed. I never did. She was smashing. Never in my life seen cleavage to rival hers. She passed your parents' stringent tests for what a future Halliburton bride ought to be. She looked great in tennis whites and was a far better sailor than you can hope to be. But, for the record, I was the one who told you not to move in with her.'

Damien bowed to his friend in agreement.

'Now,' Caleb said, 'it's been a good month since you moved

out of her place and back into the land of the sane. Time to get back on the horse.'

'Caleb, I was with Bonnie for two and a half years, while you've never dated anyone for more than a month. You're no better than a horse.'

Caleb threw his hands in the air. 'Fine. All I'm saying is, if you stop practising, one day you might wake up and realise you've forgotten how to use it.'

'Is this where I pipe in and say it's like riding a bike?'

'If you think that, then I fear Bonnie did a worse number on you than I imagined.'

Damien turned away. Bonnie hadn't done anything wrong. She'd taken their relationship at face value and assumed he was committed to the long haul. He was the bad guy. He'd been the one to walk out on her when he'd realised in playing house he'd only been kidding them both.

'But this one is fantastic,' Caleb said, all but salivating over Ms G-string.

'She's a teenager.'

'You're a killjoy.'

'You're a pig.' Damien glanced back at the wiggling backside. As far as invitations went, it was pretty clear. Caleb couldn't be entirely held to blame. So he added, 'Of course, if the G-string had been hot-pink...'

She stood and held out his goods. 'This is them?'

He glanced at the long black coat and wide, flat, silver and black mobile phone. 'That's them.'

She cocked her hip against the desk, and glanced at Caleb. 'How about you, honey? Anything here for you?'

Damien laughed out loud, before grabbing his friend by the jacket sleeve and dragging him from the restaurant and into the fresh air.

'You're not just a killjoy, you're also plain mean,' Caleb said.

'You work for me. And despite your darker predilections, you are this town's greatest shark when it comes to attracting new clients, therefore you make me lots of money, thus keeping me in the manner to which I've become accustomed. So think of me as the guy keeping you out of jail and in gainful employ.'

'Whatever.' Caleb cricked his neck, and stretched out his shoulders before heading street side to hail a cab.

Damien slid his arms into his coat and in the same move glanced back through the windows hoping to get one last look at the one woman who had created a stir within what he'd thought had been a pretty impenetrable fortress of anti-female sentiment he'd managed to cling to since leaving Bonnie high and dry.

After a few seconds he found her. Dark skirt, pale knit top, the dangerous-looking heel of her right boot bobbing up and down rhythmically. Long, silky, caramel-blonde hair cascading down her back in soft waves.

While the whole room reeked of clashing perfume and aftershave and money, she smelled like… Something soft and homey. Talcum powder? And when he'd talked to her of sunshine the word had just appeared from some deep, dark, murky, poetic place inside him he wasn't sure he needed to know existed. But the second she'd landed in his arms it had been as though a ray of light had shone through the window of the city restaurant and brightened the dank autumn day.

For a guy who'd only recently managed to extricate himself from the claws of a woman he'd thought perfectly amiable and in tune with his own life timetable, but who'd turned out to have a ticking internal clock the size of a three-bedroom suburban house, he was pretty captivated by this woman.

That alone should have made him run a mile. His conscience

still smarted at the way he'd led Bonnie on, even if it had been unintentional. But he didn't run. Instead he watched Little Miss Sunshine lift a forkful of strawberry pancakes to her lips.

It had been a month, longer really, since he'd been that physically close to a woman. All that purely feminine warmth wrapped in a package tall enough to look him in the eye in her high heels. And she had looked him in the eye. Dead on. Direct. With the golden eyes of a lioness.

He turned around to see Caleb waving his arm like a maniac as he unsuccessfully tried to hail a cab. So he went back to watching the caramel-blonde fingering a double string of tiny gold beads around her neck.

He let himself wonder if *she* owned a hot-pink lace G-string. He imagined what it would look like wrapped around her slight curves like a picture frame, no stockings, leaving the lean length from her hips to the tops of those sexy boots naked so that a man could slide his hand beneath her skirt and touch warm, bare skin...

'You coming?' Caleb called.

Damien blinked and turned from the restaurant window to find Caleb halfway into a yellow cab. He cleared his throat when he realised he wasn't in the frame of mind to sit. 'You take it. I'll walk. I have a new client near Flinders I hoped to see in person today anyway.'

'Fine. Whatever.' And Caleb was gone in a screech of burning rubber.

Damien glanced back into the restaurant one more time, but his view was obstructed by a table of newcomers, more clones in black skirt suits and glossy hair and no doubt lashings of perfume, hugging and kissing cheeks and discussing how to lock unsuspecting men into matrimony.

The lure of the female abruptly and thankfully negated, he

drew his coat tight about his neck, looked upward to find the earlier rain had already stopped and stepped out into the teeming morning city foot traffic.

'Are you going to finish those pancakes?' Kensey asked after the 'who's the hottest guy on *Grey's Anatomy*' argument had hit a lull. 'I'm starving. Probably because I'm pregnant.'

Chelsea let her fork drop to her plate. 'Did you just say that you're—?'

'Up the duff,' Kensey said. 'With child. Bun in the oven. I did. I am.'

Chelsea's gaze slid across the table to Kensey's large water glass, not the usual fancy-looking cocktail heavy with tiny paper umbrellas or pink plastic flamingos she ordered any time she had an adult meal without her kids in tow.

'Wow. But didn't Greg just have the…?' Chelsea mimed a pair of scissors.

'They did tell us it doesn't work right away, takes a few weeks to be sure. But it was our anniversary, and we were both in the mood, and the kids were all asleep by nine.'

Well what do you know? Kensey was pregnant with her *fourth*. The crazy number that meant she needed a people mover and extensions to the holiday hut in the Yarra Valley they could barely afford. It meant chaos. Yet Kensey looked so sublimely happy. Chelsea felt an unexpected surge of bitter-sweet envy form in her veins.

'How far along are you?' she asked.

'Eight weeks, give or take.' Kensey let out a long shaky breath and Chelsea realised this was half the reason behind the big fancy breakfast and she'd been so tunnel-visioned about her own issues. She was a bad sister. 'I have no idea how we are going to do this.'

'You'll be fine. You guys are always fine.'

Kensey grabbed Chelsea by both hands. 'If you believe in my judgment so much, then let me find you a man of your own so we can have babies together. Imagine a brood with dark hair and blue eyes like that Mr Handsome burning love from earlier.'

'Whoa there, partner. You're the one who ended up with the white-picket-fence gene while I got the modicum-of-business-sense gene. Both miracles considering our parentage. Besides, can you imagine that guy coming anywhere near the Pride & Groom? He'd be covered in white dog hair the minute the door let in the slightest gust of wind. Karma would crucify me for daring to mar such perfection.'

'Well, so long as it's something of great magnitude keeping you from grabbing such a man with both hands. What was wrong with the last guy again?'

'Gay,' Chelsea shot back.

'Okay, so maybe your reasons for sending your menagerie of admirers on their merry way are becoming more sensible over time. Less like purposeful sabotage. By the time you're in your fifties you'll give some poor guy a break when you finally realise they are not all deadbeats like Dad.'

Chelsea glared at her sister as she grabbed her plate back. 'Maybe I will finish those pancakes after all. And I sincerely hope you're having triplets.'

Damien's mobile phone chirped melodiously.

He vaguely recognised the ring tone as the theme song from some girly TV show. *The Gilmore Girls? Laverne and Shirley?* Bloody Caleb must have been mucking around with it at some stage that morning.

'Halliburton,' he answered in a clipped tone as he checked

the street for traffic before jogging across in front of a slow-moving taxi.

'Ah, hi,' a hesitant female voice said. 'Is this the Pride & Groom salon?'

'Nope. Sorry. Wrong number.' He snapped the phone shut. And moved into the stream of pedestrian traffic heading uptown.

The phone rang again. This time he recognised it instantly as the theme from *The Mary Tyler Moore Show*. Bloody *bloody* Caleb. In a fit of guilt he'd let Bonnie keep the lease on his old apartment and been living with his best friend ever since. He really would have to get off his friend's couch very soon.

'Halliburton,' he answered.

This time there was a pause. 'I am calling for Letitia Forbes from the special features desk of *Chic* magazine,' the hesitant female voice said once more. 'Is Chelsea London nearby?'

Damien pulled up short. He turned to look over his shoulder to see if perhaps this was some kind of joke and Caleb was following at an indiscreet distance. But all he saw was a wall of people looking as drab as the grey sky above. He slipped out of the stream and ensconced himself against the window of a comic-book shop.

'I'm in Melbourne, Ms Forbes. London is on the other side of the planet.'

'I know where Chelsea, the place, is. I'm looking for Chelsea London, the proprietor of the Pride & Groom salon. This was the phone number I was supplied.'

'Apologies. Still can't help. I am the proprietor of a day trading institution, Keppler Jones and Morganstern, this is my number and all I know of *Chic* is that my little sister used to hide it from my mum when she was fourteen.'

Letitia Forbes' assistant laughed a pretty tinkly laugh that was all flirtation and no substance. Damien appreciated it for what it was, but it did nothing to move him. Not like when the caramel-blonde had blinked up at him with her golden eyes and made him give in and slide his hands that much further around her waist, lean in that much closer to capture the scent of her hair…

He closed his eyes to squeeze out the unwelcome wave of pure lust swarming over him.

'So what do you know of animal-print dog collars?' Letitia Forbes' assistant asked.

His eyes flew back open. 'Because…?'

'That's why I'm trying to track down Chelsea London. For her professional opinion. But I'm now wondering if your opinion might be just as valid.'

He checked his watch. This day was fast slipping away from him. 'Unfortunately my only experience with animal-print anything has been with the underwear variety.'

'Yours?' she asked.

'That I cannot say for fear I might incriminate myself.'

She paused, and he sensed she was searching for a way to keep him on the line. With a sigh she said, 'Alas I have other phone calls to make, hopefully with as much fun but more success. Good day to you, Mr Halliburton.'

'Same to you.' He snapped the phone shut and stared at it for a few seconds as the world continued to walk on by.

Right. So in the past hour he'd had a woman fall into his arms, one flash her G-string at him, another whisper a suggestion in his ear that would have been more fitting for a key party, and yet another flirt him into intimating he was wearing zebra-print undies beneath his trousers.

For all the female attention he was getting today it was as if the women around him had some kind of radar. The only time in his thirty-two years on this planet he *wasn't* seeking out any kind of co-ed companionship, it took no kind of effort on his part to have it rolling towards him in waves.

Women... he thought. *Can't live with them...*

He glanced up, caught the eye of an elderly lady with tight purple ringlets. She smiled, and blushed. He wondered if he ought to head straight back to Amelie's and ask exactly what they'd put into his hollandaise sauce.

But even as he thought it he knew it wasn't the sauce. Sure, he was easy enough on the eye, had means, skills and other intangible assets that seemed to appeal to more women than not, but what was happening to him today was something other. Something primal. And it had begun the moment the woman of all things warm and sunny had fallen into his arms and set his pheromones alight.

Since then he'd been on some sort of constant sexual high. Walking, talking and acting like a normal person, but only half his mind was on real life. The other half had been replaying the memory of the most subtle scent that somehow took him back to a simpler time when all he'd wanted from life was a hug and a kiss before bedtime. Perhaps if he just stopped thinking about *her* he could get back to work without being mobbed in the street by a hundred ready-dressed brides.

His phone rang again and he flinched like a spooked school-boy. He took a deep calming breath and this time waited to see if his address book recognised the phone number. It did. 'Letitia @ Chic Mag,' it read.

Sure, it was one of those computer/organiser/mobile whiz-bang things that cost a small fortune, but as far as he knew it didn't have any kind of cognitive memory. Unless he'd saved those details they shouldn't be there.

He continued staring at his phone as it played out *The Mary*

Tyler Moore Show theme. Once it rang out, he flipped it open and found himself staring at the large inner screen, which instead of a plain font espousing the name of his mobile phone company had an animated picture of a pink paw-print.

The truth finally dawned.

It was not his phone.

Damien slowly flipped the phone closed and breathed deep through his nose, gaining a lungful of car exhaust and day-old garbage for his effort.

How could he not have known it wasn't his phone? Real men loved their electronic toys more than life itself. Hell, every other guy he knew surrounded themselves with 5.1 surround sound, sub-woofers, and fancy walkmans with earplugs and wireless remote who knew what.

When he'd been talked into trading in his trusty five-year-old Nokia with its comforting scratches and dents for some top of the range gadget, he'd been told it would change his life. And now it had. Right now he had no idea of the address or phone number for the new clients he was hoping to meet, and he had a ring tone that made him seem far from manly.

'Dammit!' he said loud enough several people took a wider berth around him.

He reached into his trouser pocket and there was the hot-pink ticket for *his* phone, meaning the one he'd found on the floor behind his chair just as he'd left Amelie's hadn't been his.

The phone was thankfully unlocked, so he dialled his old friend Directory Assistance. 'Amelie's Brasserie, Melbourne,' he requested when a voice with a light foreign accent answered.

He saw a gap in the traffic between a tram and oncoming cars and jogged back across the wide street where he found a cab, slipped inside and gave directions back to his Collins Street office.

Amelie's answered.

'Damien Halliburton here. I breakfasted with you guys today and managed to pick up the wrong phone.' He pulled the phone away from his ear for a second to get the attention of the cab driver. 'Left onto Russell will be quicker this time of day.'

He waited for the grovelling and simpering on the other end of the phone to die down before interjecting, 'Can you check box J? It's empty? Right.'

Plan B. Which was…

Perhaps he ought to get the cabbie to make a sharp turn and get him back there a.s.a.p. so that he could search for it himself. And if the caramel-blonde happened to still be there he could also…what?

He glanced at his watch. No time. And the gent on the other end of the phone was talking again.

'Don't bother,' Damien said. 'I'll sort it out myself.'

He snapped the phone shut tight. It made a softer, more worn-in sound than his did, meaning it belonged to someone who would be missing it. Christy something or other. No, Chelsea. Chelsea London. An apparent expert on zebra-print dog collars. He couldn't have had the same type of phone as another executive type with big muscles and an even bigger stock portfolio, could he? No, it had to be some broad with parents who should be shot for giving her such an unforgivable name.

The cab pulled up outside the imposing thirty-storey building that housed the Keppler Jones and Morganstern Trading Company. He tossed the driver a twenty and hit the ground running.

Chelsea kissed Kensey goodbye at the cloakroom at Amelie's and stood watching her sister walk away with a lightness in her step.

Kensey's news was lovely. Despite their erratic and fly-by-night childhood her sister had made good and then some. They both had. There was really nothing for Chelsea to be feeling this edgy about.

'Your ticket, ma'am,' a girl behind the counter said.

'Right.' Chelsea searched her handbag. The pockets of her jacket. Down her bra where she often slipped notes to herself when she didn't have her phone or pockets to hand. She glanced up to find the blonde watching her blankly.

'I seem to have misplaced it.'

'It'll be hot-pink. Hard to miss.'

'Yet visualising it still hasn't helped it appear.'

The blonde raised an eyebrow. Chelsea took a deep breath and managed to count to seven before she leant over the counter and said, 'It's black. With a silver spine, off-white buttons, and if you flip it open it will have this picture upon the screen.'

She slipped the blonde a Pride & Groom business card with the hot-pink dog-print logo upon it. The blonde took the card and then her right eyebrow joined her left.

'Cool. You work for those guys?'

'I am those guys.'

'Ri-i-ight. Weren't you on the telly a few months back? On that celebrity pet show? You're the one who clipped that rock star's poodle and he freaked out that you'd swapped his dog, and sued you.'

The rock star had threatened to sue, had been appeased by the show's producers that the dog was his just with a haircut, and by the next day couldn't even remember a word of it. Pride & Groom's business had doubled overnight, making Chelsea believe whoever said all publicity was good publicity deserved a cookie. 'I am the very one,' she agreed.

The blonde tipped her chin and looked up at Chelsea from

beneath clumpy eyelashes. 'I have a Basenji. Any chance you could swing me some freebies?'

Chelsea blinked back. 'Any chance you could find my phone? Black, silver, off-white keys…'

The blonde smirked and ran a finger along the wooden boxes until she found the only one that was locked. She pulled out Chelsea's black and silver friend. 'This it?'

Chelsea slid it out of the girl's hand and wrapped her fingers around the familiar length, comfort seeping into her joints at having her life somewhat back under her control. 'This is it.'

'Any time you need a table at short notice, just ask for Carrie. That's me.'

'Thanks, Carrie. I'll keep it in mind.'

The give and take of commerce, Chelsea thought as she snuck a knee-length wool scarf from her handbag and wrapped it twice around her neck and headed outside into the crisp, but at least now dry, Melbourne autumn morning. *Luck out with the right product and today you were on everybody's speed dial. Dream too big in the slight wrong direction and tomorrow you're toast.*

She pulled her hair out from under her tight scarf as she headed down the street towards the underground car park where she'd left the Pride & Groom van.

And promptly began dreaming big in the exact wrong direction. Each footstep heralded the memory of another delicious moment locked in the arms of a tall dark handsome stranger from so far on the other side of the tracks he was in a different postcode.

And Kensey had made a point that had hit deep.

She was twenty-seven years old. Self-sufficient. Post puppy fat and pre middle-aged spread. She could still touch her toes and her hair had yet to turn mousy. These were meant to be her golden years, yet the only man she'd purposely dressed up for in weeks was the bank manager.

She felt a sudden desire to turn on her high heels, march back into the restaurant and ask the blonde if she could find out the booking name and phone number of Mr Suit and Tie. Even though he'd been too beautiful for her, too beautiful for anyone bar maybe three or four of the world's top supermodels, he'd looked at her as if…as if he'd wanted to see more of her.

The way his arms had tightened around her, the way his gorgeous blue eyes had darkened, made her feel that having a man like him hold her, touch her, bury himself in her, call out her name, even just the once, would be some kind of validation that she was young and single and would be perfectly fine if life deemed she remain that way evermore.

But then again, if she ever had the chance to experience such a dreamy specimen, would she, being of London genes, find it impossible to appreciate ordinary pleasures ever again?

CHAPTER THREE

DAMIEN burst into Caleb's office without knocking. 'Don't laugh or I *will* hit you.'

Caleb didn't laugh. He was too busy running a lazy hand through his short hair while a tall lean blonde straightened her skirt. She gave Damien a quick smile before sliding out the office door and shutting it behind her.

'Do I know her?' Damien drawled.

'Zelda's from the typing pool. She was replacing my printer cartridge.'

Damien nodded. 'That was nice of her. But how about you stick to looking after your own printer cartridges while in the workplace? My workplace. For which I am legally liable. Now, I need your help.'

Caleb sat back in his chair and leant his chin on steepled fingers. 'What's up, boss?'

'You know how I suggested we try Amelie's because they don't let anyone use their mobile phones? How I railed that it might well become the one place in this city where a man could eat in relative peace?'

Caleb nodded, feigning deep understanding, though when he leaned forward and started fiddling with the mouse on his desk Damien knew he had to be quick.

'In some kind of karmic response to my admittedly anti-technology sentiments, when I picked up my phone from the cloakroom, they gave me the wrong one.'

Caleb glanced up at the phone Damien held by his fingertips. 'Looks like yours.'

'But it ain't.'

'But it looks like it...'

Just then the offending machine began to ring. The two men stared at it as it blared out its powder-puff tune.

'That's not your phone,' Caleb said, deadpan. 'Give it to me.'

Damien pulled it out of Caleb's reach. 'Every time you go anywhere near my computer I end up with porn pop-ups I have to call on others to delete. Now every Friday for the past two months Jimmy the IT guy has asked me if I want to join him and the other techies at the Men's Gallery.'

'I can't put porn on this phone by simply answering it.' Caleb clicked his fingers, and, half believing him, Damien handed over the offending instrument.

'This is Caleb,' he said after answering the phone, leaning back in his chair, and proceeding to ask sensible questions. When Caleb's voice dropped and he began to have a chat, Damien kicked hard against the side of his desk.

'Right, nice talking to you, Susan,' Caleb said, then hung up. 'She was returning a missed call herself. Didn't know whose phone it was. If you'd let me talk for a few more minutes we might have figured it out between us.'

'Nevertheless.'

'I think it's a chick's phone,' Caleb said.

'I do believe it is. Someone rang earlier looking for a Chelsea London.'

'Now why do I know that name?'

'You don't,' Damien said, knowing that Caleb wouldn't spot the obvious.

Caleb grinned. 'You bought a chick's phone.'

'On your recommendation.'

'That was a month ago. Times change. I can't see the future.'

'I wonder what they did with my old one. Do you think it's too late to get it back?'

'Far too late. If they haven't melted it down they've donated it to a museum.' Caleb's thumb began zooming over the keys at lightning speed.

'You're going through her personal files?' Damien asked.

'That I am.'

'Good idea.' He moved behind Caleb and looked over his shoulder at the bright flashing screens.

'No photos of herself or her friends. Means she has no friends or isn't the cutest thing on her block. But we do have photos of…'

Damien's eyebrows lifted and he was sure Caleb's did the same. The first photo they came upon was of a black studded dog collar. He should have guessed.

'Kinky,' Caleb said.

'Just your type,' Damien said.

'Ha. Ha. Okay, moving on, in her diary we have "breakfast @ Amelie's with Kensey". Kensey. Sounds like the name of a fortune-teller. Ooh, maybe this Kensey knows what they've done with your old phone.'

Damien closed his eyes for a moment. 'So now what?'

Caleb held up the phone to the light pouring through the office window as though that could make it magically ring again. 'What happened when you called your phone number to see if this Chelsea chick has your phone?'

Damien squeezed his eyes shut all the tighter as he mentally berated himself. The caramel-blonde had done more than awoken his dormant hungers; it seemed she'd also dulled his brain cells in the process. That had never happened to him after *not* having seen a woman he was keen on naked. In fact, he couldn't remember feeling such debilitating mind fuzz upon actually seeing a woman he was keen on naked.

It occurred to him in some kind of cruel flash of remembrance that he'd even remained focussed in every which way during the worst of the fights leading to the eventual Break Up. Bonnie had declared him a dyed-in-the-wool Halliburton incapable of a committed relationship other than with his work. And he hadn't even thought to argue.

Damien looked at his watch. The markets had been open almost an hour and he'd not placed one trade for a client. So much for his impassioned commitment to his work. He clicked his fingers, and Caleb handed over the phone.

He pressed it to his ear and paced to the window, looking out over the Melbourne city skyline. The now bright blue skies streaked with perfect fluffy white clouds mocked him as the phone buzzed ominously in his ear.

Just as Chelsea pulled into a parking garage beneath the imposing Brunswick Street building, the phone on the passenger seat began to vibrate so vigorously it almost fell off the seat.

She jumped in fright. She never used vibrate. Her phone was far too important for all that silent-mode nonsense. She made a mental note to write to the restaurant and let them know their cloakroom staff had been mucking about with her ring tone.

She grabbed it, and her bag, and leapt out of the van. She screened the call. Her right foot slid to a stop in a pile of white gravel when her own mobile number looked back at her.

She glanced about her. Hippies, Goths, punks and innumerable other marginal folk who gravitated to the funky urban *je ne sais quoi* of inner city Brunswick Street brushed past her on the pavement, but she saw nothing in any of their faces to help her make sense of her current situation.

Her tone was more than a mite cautious when she flipped the phone open and said, 'Chelsea London speaking.'

After a pause, a deep male voice said, 'Chelsea London, am I glad to have found you.'

She began walking again, this time more slowly. 'Who is this?'

'My name is Damien Halliburton. I'm a day trader with Keppler Jones and Morganstern.'

A day trader, she computed. Was that some kind of market-research thing? Ooh, she hated those guys! Phone calls just as she'd settled down to lasagne, red wine and *House.* Though at least this one's voice was something out of the ordinary. Booming deep, slow and easy, like really good pillow talk.

God! Was her mind now permanently switched to hot, naked, sweaty mode?

She shook her head and pressed the phone tighter to her ear so Mr Pillow Talk could feel the full force of her disappointment that a man with a voice like his had taken on such a job.

'Mr Keppler-Jones or Morganwhoever, I never answer surveys, never tick the "please send me more information" boxes on forms. Didn't you know that Australia's privacy laws actually refer to you as well as the rest of the population?'

After a distinct pause, which she saw as something of a victory, especially since he was likely being graded and re-corded by a boss with a clipboard, he said, 'I think you may have me mistaken for somebody else, Ms London.'

Ms London? That settled it. This guy didn't know her from Eve. She stopped atop the front porch of the large white building and crossed her spare arm over her stomach. 'Right. So how the hell do you have my phone number?'

'I have more than that,' the deep voice said. 'I have your phone.'

She pulled the phone out from its nook between her shoulder and her chin as though it had emitted an electrical charge. She stared at it. Black. Silver spine. Glowing off-white buttons.

She ducked inside. Only when she glanced through the glass door at the street outside did she tuck the phone back beneath her chin. She picked up only what must have been the end of his next sentence.

'...Amelie's today?'

Amelie's? Was he some kind of crazy stalker?

'Whoever you are, call me again and I will be onto the police before you can take your next heavy breath.'

With that she hung up, and threw the phone into her handbag. Then she took a deep breath and marched up to the service desk at the local bank. 'I'm Chelsea London. I have an appointment to see your manager about a business loan.'

Damien held the phone away from his ear and stared at it for several blank seconds.

'All sorted?' Caleb asked.

'Well, no. Not exactly. I think she may in fact be a crazy lady.'

'The dog-collar photo didn't ring those bells for ya? Maybe she stole your phone on purpose,' Caleb said. 'Maybe this is something she does to get her kicks.'

Damien redialled. After several rings it went through to his voicemail. 'She's not answering.'

'Maybe she's on the phone again. Maybe she's calling her

crazy relatives overseas. On your dime. That's her con! So who do you know overseas we could call at this time of day?'

Damien didn't wait to hear the end of it. He simply upped and left Caleb's office and walked down the hall to his own, wondering whom he'd hurt in a previous existence in order to have so very many women adding unnecessary pressures to what, until a month ago, had been the kind of easy, breezy, fortunate life most men would give their right arm for.

An hour and a bit later, Chelsea trudged inside the converted house in which the first Pride & Groom salon had grown from a one-woman, one-van operation into a brand-recognised, seven-staff, three-van endeavour with room for up to half a dozen domestic animals to be washed, clipped, perfumed, primped, preened and pampered at once.

She threw her handbag onto the white cane tub chair in the corner of her tiny office, her muscles aching as if she'd carried her own body weight from the car. Though all she'd done was carry a couple of dozen pieces of paper, which basically said if she signed them she'd owe the bank somewhere in the region of a million dollars.

She kicked off her boots, then licked her finger and rubbed it hard over a spot of strawberry sauce on her top, which had thankfully been hidden beneath her jacket.

She then changed into her more comfortable 'uniform' of faded jeans, long-sleeved white T-shirt with a big hot-pink paw print splodged dead centre, and thick socks to stave off blisters associated with being on her feet all day.

As she sat to tie up the laces on her sneakers the office door burst open and Phyllis stuck her head in. 'Well, now, where the heck you been? I must have tried to call you a good half-dozen times. Kept getting your voicemail.'

'Sorry. Phone was on silent.' For once. The last thing she'd needed was crazy stalker telemarketer man bombarding her whilst she and the bank manager had been chatting.

Phyllis leaned her heavy form against the door frame. 'So how did we go?'

'It's all ours if we want it. Enough money to buy and fit out another two salons.'

Phyllis let out a resounding whoop. 'I knew it. You clever *clever* girl. Now, just a quick warning. The Joneses brought Pumpkin in this morning and she seems to have a slight, okay not so slight, tummy upset. She has had it all over the green room, in fact. Lily's on lunch. Josie gags every time she walks past the room. And I would clean up but I have Agatha's Burmese and if I leave her alone for another two minutes you know she'll turn feral.'

Chelsea let her sneaker-clad foot drop to the floor with a thud. It seemed her pretend life as a sophisticated city gal with a million dollars to spend and sexy city-banker types drooling over her was well and truly over. 'Call the Joneses. Ask if they'd like us to take Pumpkin to Dr Campbell. Then give me a few minutes and I'll clean it up.'

Phyllis left. Chelsea pushed up her sleeves and tied her hair back into a pony-tail. She fished her mobile out of her bag and placed it on a spare corner of her desk, which was overflowing with trays filled with 'to do' lists, samples of dog-grooming products that arrived in the mail every day, and a just-short-of-stale half-packet of shortbread that would be morning tea.

She stared out the small window into the rose garden next door, her eyes fuzzing over as she watched a bee flit from flower to flower. And her thoughts once again turned to Mr Suit and Tie.

She wondered if he wasn't what he'd seemed at first glance

either. Perhaps right now he was pulling on a pair of overalls, or pulling off his shirt and tie to reveal superhero Lycra beneath. Or maybe he was still dressed in glorious top-to-toe suiting, leaning back in a thousand-dollar chair, counting his money and laughing maniacally at the little men pedalling hard to make his privileged world go round.

Damien sat forward in his chair, the soft swish and swing of German engineering making him bob comfortably behind his oak and leather desk.

Far more comfortably than he deserved, as his day was still occurring in slow motion since his hormones had mutinously overtaken his higher brain function. All because of a willowy body so light in his arms he could have swung her around and not done his back in, golden-brown eyes, pale warm skin, tumbling waves he'd never had the chance to touch.

He needed to give himself a break. A man and a woman taking pleasure in one another and leaving it at that wasn't unheard of in this day and age. And if it couldn't be her it would have to be someone else and soon. If only he had her number.

His gaze slid to the mobile phone on his desk, which had not stopped singing about Mary Bloody Tyler Moore all bloody morning.

He rubbed his eyes again, shook his head until his brain rattled inside his skull, then placed his fingers over the keys and clicked on the next email.

Then Caleb sauntered into his office and Damien wondered then and there if the time had come to simply call it quits and go find a nice warm bar somewhere to hole up for the duration.

'So, at the bank today…' Kensey's voice crackled through the landline phone tucked between Chelsea's ear and shoulder.

'I'm approved. Though I haven't signed the papers.'

'Chels!'

'I know. I know. It's a great opportunity. But it's such a huge gamble.'

Kensey paused, making sure she was listening. 'This isn't some pie-in-the-sky get-rich-quick fantasy like Dad would have taken on.'

'You're right,' Chelsea said. 'I'll sign them. I'll probably sign them. Later.'

She flipped open her mobile with one hand and stared at the screen as she had been incessantly for the past minute. There was still no Pride & Groom logo where a logo should be. 'Now as I was saying, this isn't my mobile.'

'So whose is it?'

'If I knew that I'd be talking to them right now and not you.'

The phone suddenly began vibrating in her hand. She whispered, 'It's ringing.'

Kensey finished chewing what sounded like dry biscuits, then said, 'I can hold.'

'No, not this phone, the other phone. The evil impostor phone.' She screened the call, to find her own number looking back at her again. 'Hang on, I'll put you on speaker in case it's the market research guy and he threatens me again.'

She hurriedly put down the landline, tentatively picked up the mobile, and answered. 'Hello?'

'Chelsea London?' the same clear, deep masculine voice from earlier asked.

'This is she.'

'This is Damien Halliburton again. Don't hang up. Please.'

'I'm listening.'

'Did you dine at Amelie's earlier today?'

'I did.'

'Well, then, Chelsea, I do believe there was some kind of mix-up in the cloakroom. I've been forced to relive *The Mary Tyler Moore Show* more times today than I thought I would have to during the rest of my life. Sound familiar?'

'It does.' It also made more sense than the stalker alternative. Chelsea blushed furiously as Kensey's laughter trickled through her speaker phone.

'Then the mystery is solved. We have one another's phones. So how about you give me your address and I can send a cab—'

'Lord no!' Chelsea shot back. 'I'm not sure how close you are to your phone, but mine contains my whole life. Sticking it in a dark pigeon-hole in that rotten restaurant was bad enough. I don't want it out of safe hands again.'

'Okay,' he said. 'So I guess we meet. Swap. Go our merry ways.'

'Much better.' Chelsea remembered the Joneses' dog with the tummy bug. 'I'm afraid I'm stuck at work. Can you come to me? I'm in Fitzroy.'

'I'm in the city. And considering I've spent the past hour trying to figure out what happened I'm more than a tad behind on my work for the day.'

'Right. So when could we make this happen?'

'How about we meet at seven back at Amelie's?'

Her lip curled at the thought of returning to the place. But it made sense. 'How will we find one another?'

'It's typical for the man to wear a rose in his lapel.'

Her right eyebrow shot skyward even though he wasn't there to see it. 'This is a business transaction, Mr Halliburton. Not a blind date.'

He cleared his throat. 'So it is.'

'Hey, Chels,' Kensey's voice blurted from the speaker phone.

'Hang on a sec,' Chelsea said to the guy. And then to Kensey, 'What?'

'Send each other a picture.'

'What?'

'On your phones.'

Brilliant! She knew she had a sister for a reason.

'Mr Halliburton, did you get that?' Chelsea asked.

A pause. Muffled voices. Was he checking with his own partner in crime at the other end? Could this day get any stranger?

He finally said, 'How does one do that?'

Chelsea blinked. 'My phone is exactly the same as yours.'

'Now might be the time to admit something to you.'

'And that would be…'

'I have no skills in the electronics area. Can't even program a VCR.'

'Lucky nobody makes VCRs any more. It's all about the DVD hard drive.'

'And there I was wondering why my *Rocky* tape wouldn't fit in the slot.'

Chelsea realised she was grinning. Now that she knew he wasn't a stalker, she could appreciate the sense of humour that came with the lovely deep voice. 'How charming. You're a Luddite.'

'Card-carrying,' he said.

'So get Keppler-Jones or Morganwhoever to give you a hand.'

'Two of them are dead, and one's so old he ought to be. And they've left the idiots to run the asylum.'

'You?'

He laughed down the phone, the sound vibrating across radio waves, through metal and down her arm until she gave into the need to scratch her elbow.

'Nice of you to make that leap so fast. But yes. And lucky for me I have hired well and have someone nearby who I'm sure would have used a photo function on a phone more often than entirely necessary.'

'Excellent.'

Chelsea knew she ought to sign off and get to work, but all she had waiting for her was goodness knew what gastronomical disaster in the green room. And besides, this peculiar exchange was turning out to be fun. Risk-free, anonymous fun, which was the kind she was more than happy to indulge in. So instead she asked, 'Um, perhaps we ought to keep note of any phone calls that come through to our respective phones too.'

'Right. Sorry, I should have mentioned you did have a couple of calls from…ah, *Chic* magazine, earlier.'

'*Chic?*' Chelsea clenched a fist in happiness. She had been waiting on confirmation that they wanted her to host a two-page spread on celebrity pet accessories. If she wanted a platform from which to announce a possible expansion… 'I do believe you just made my day.'

'I take it they're not chasing you down to pay up on a new subscription, then.'

'Ah, no.' This time the grin came with an accompanying laugh, which after the uneasiness that marred her morning felt as good as an hour-long Swedish massage followed by a bubble bath.

'And when you get back to *Chic* to explain why I was not you, if they mention anything about my predilection for zebra-print underwear they're making the whole thing up.'

Chelsea slowly leant back in her chair and began to play with her hair. 'I'm not sure *Chic* are in the habit of spreading rumours like that about random guys.'

'It's a scandal. Best kept under wraps for all our sakes.'

He paused again. She took a long breath and let it go, the release flowing from her cheeks all the way to her toes.

'So, any messages for me?' he asked, and his voice dropped lower. She felt it like a hum in her very centre. Like a warm glow building so slowly her fingers and toes felt cold in comparison.

She sat up straight and curled her toes in her shoes until the blood returned.

Bloody Kensey's pregnancy, she thought, *and, worse yet, rotten Mr Suit and Tie.* He was the real reason the voice on the other end of the phone was making her feel warm and fuzzy. She was like a light bulb that couldn't be turned off. Even the married loan manager at the bank had tried to flirt with her.

'Ah, no,' she said, clearing her throat. 'The only phone call I've had was from some guy who claimed to have kidnapped my phone.'

'I hope you told him where to go.'

She laughed again despite herself. 'In no uncertain terms.'

'That's my girl.'

They both paused again, conversation suddenly, sadly, exhausted.

Chelsea sat forward again, and shook her fringe off her cheeks. 'So…we do it now? Send the photos, and see you at seven?'

'Chelsea London,' he said, 'consider it a date.'

And before she had the chance to remind him that it was a five-second phone-swap, and no lapel roses would be necessary, he was gone. She slid the phone shut. Slowly.

'Humona humona,' Kensey said and Chelsea jumped halfway out of her skin, having forgotten her sister was still on speaker phone.

'I'm sorry? *Humona* what?'

'I could feel the sparks from here. I think he likes you. And for this one you don't even need to ask for his number! You know it off by heart.'

'Kensey…' she warned.

'He had a great voice,' Kensey said. 'Like Irish cream liqueur: creamy smooth and, oh, so bad for your balance unless in very small doses. Call him back. Or, better yet, call Amelie's and book a table for seven and casually ask him to stay for dinner when you meet up.'

'I can't! What if he's some kind of crazy? Or if he's eighteen years old? Or married? Or brings his imaginary friend to the table? Or smells like fish? Or hates dogs?'

'Or is tall, dark and handsome and this whole phone-swap deal was a sign from the gods.'

Oh, no. Chelsea was pretty sure she'd been given her fair share of tall, dark and handsome strangers this day.

'So what picture are you going to send?' Kensey asked.

'Oh, um, I guess I'll just snap one off now and—'

'Nuh-uh. Those things are such bad quality. The kids are still in school for another couple of hours. I'm coming over. I'll help you come up with something sweet with just a hint of slutty.'

'Kensey…' Chelsea said, for what must have been the tenth time that day.

'Don't argue. Besides, we haven't finished the bank-loan conversation yet. See you in fifteen minutes,' Kensey said and then was gone.

For a moment Chelsea wished for simpler times when keeping one's front door shut was enough of an excuse not to have to make contact with another soul.

CHAPTER FOUR

AFTER what felt like an age later, a soft tinkling sound like a wind chime shifting in a light breeze heralded the arrival of a picture on the mobile phone in Damien's hand.

'Let me do the honours,' Caleb begged.

'Not on your life.'

'I have to see what the kinky cat lady looks like.'

'Now she's a cat lady?'

'I'm picturing a sari-wearer. Maybe even bald. Hurry up and check. I'm dying here.'

She sure hadn't sounded like a bald cat lady. She'd sounded…lovely. Likely because every woman he'd come in contact with since The Caramel-Blonde had turned into a purring temptress as though he were wearing a sign around his neck saying: *Newly single. On the market. Fresh meat.*

Maybe what he needed was a long holiday. Somewhere warm. And isolated. Palm trees, coconuts, no women, and no mobile-phone coverage. But excellent computer facilities and air-conditioning and twenty-hour working days.

He flipped open the phone, hoping that was all he'd have to do to determine whom he had to find in several hours time. Then he'd get back to work like a good little business owner.

The picture formed on the screen. He blinked. And blinked

again. A swell of heat poured like lava through his midriff as his eyes roved over silky hair the colour of rich caramel, delicate cheekbones, and fine pink lips. And he would have recognised those eyes of gold in a crowd of thousands.

He landed back in his chair and swung it around to face the city beyond the great smoked-glass window in his corner office, and ran a hard hand over his chin.

'Well, what do you know?' Caleb said, breathing over his shoulder. 'The cat lady's a hottie.'

'Of course she is,' Damien spat out. 'It's *her.*'

'Her? Her who?'

'The woman from the restaurant.'

'But she was blonde and—'

'Not the G-stringed teeny bopper. The one who fell into my arms when you were in the loo. I pointed her out to you just before we left.'

Caleb looked closer. 'Bloody hell, you're right. She was hot too.'

Damien turned his chair back to face his office, dropped the phone to the desk and leant his forehead into his open palms. 'Her ticket must have fallen to the floor when she fell. I picked it up. And by all that's holy we have the same phone.'

'You lucky sod,' Caleb said. 'Now what you have to do is ring her again, tell her you have to change your appointment to later in the evening. Book a table. Get there early. Order a bottle of wine…And why aren't you writing any of this down?'

Damien shook his head. 'Because I broke up with Bonnie little more than a month ago. I can't…'

Want some stranger with such all-consuming immediacy, he'd been about to say. Instead he went with the much safer, 'I'm of the thought that it would be better for me to not indulge in such pursuits just yet.'

'I'm not suggesting you marry the girl. Or any girl, for that matter. Dinner. Cocktails. Maybe a grope in the back of the cab on the way home. Sounds like a perfectly fine Tuesday evening, if you ask me.'

Damien did his best not to let Caleb's words infiltrate. When it came to dealing with the fairer sex Caleb was a schmuck. But he certainly painted a nice picture. Her soft, soothing scent still lingered on his jacket even now. Who knew what levels of pleasure more than two minutes in one another's company might bring them? Certainly more pleasure than he'd had in some time.

'So are you going to call Amelie's or should I do it for you?'

Damien glared up at his friend. 'Don't you have work to do?'

'Slave-driver,' Caleb said.

And as soon as Caleb sauntered from Damien's office with a wink and a smile, he was on the phone to Amelie's to insist they give him a last-minute table to make up for the emotional stress they'd put him through.

Caleb wasn't often right, but this time he might have been just on the money. The time to get back on the horse was nigh.

Chelsea came back into her office after cleaning and disinfecting the green room feeling as bad as the poor Joneses' dog had looked. She was wet and bedraggled from top to toe. And she wasn't certain her shoes had managed to avoid every little surprise left on the concrete floor.

The mobile phone on her desk was buzzing and vibrating until she felt it in her fillings.

'It's been doing that for ten minutes,' Kensey said from her position on the soft window-seat in Chelsea's office, her nose buried in a catalogue of doggie accessories.

'So why don't you answer it?' Chelsea asked, pulling off her long-sleeved T-shirt and replacing it with an exact match, though one that was warmer and dryer.

'Fine,' Kensey said with a sigh, then grabbed the phone, flipped it open, and stared for a few moments, her expression so blank Chelsea began to get worried.

'What? Tell me. It's him, isn't it? Is he creepy? Is he famous? Is he my evil twin? What?'

But when Kensey began to laugh, so hard she clutched her belly and drew her knees to her chest for support, Chelsea grabbed the phone.

She stared at the picture. It was slightly askew, cutting off his left ear and showing far too much room atop his head, but the face, *that* face, was unmistakable.

Thick, dark, preppy-perfect hair. A dead straight nose. And permanently smiling blue eyes. Damien Halliburton of the creamy voice, charmingly off-kilter sense of humour, and apparent predilection for zebra-print underwear was the very man into whose arms she had fallen.

Chelsea sank into her chair with a thud. 'It's *him,* isn't it? It's really *him.*'

Kensey nodded.

'And now I have to go back there, tonight, and see *him* again.'

'You sure do.'

She glanced down at the wet patches on her old jeans, and flicked a blob of soapy hair from her cheek. 'He won't remember I'm, you know, the girl with the bad balance, will he?'

'You have been given a second chance to blind the guy with your fabulousness. Does it matter if he remembers you?'

Chelsea bit at her inner lip. In the long-suppressed, non-pragmatic, romantic, dreamy, girly places deep inside her it mattered more than she would ever admit.

'So what does Mr Gorgeous here do again?' Kensey asked.

Chelsea screwed up her nose and squinted at Kensey. 'I think he's some kind of telemarketer. For Keppler Jones and somebody.'

Kensey only laughed all the more. 'Did you pay any attention to how much our breakfast cost us today? He's no telemarketer.'

Kensey stood and bumped Chelsea aside with her hip. She leaned over the computer on the desk and typed his name and Keppler Jones into a search engine then clicked on the top listing. And up came a schmick website with all the latest Flash graphics. All creams and sky-blues and greys. Cool, sophisticated, and intimidating.

'It's a trading firm. Stocks and bonds and the like.' Kensey's nimble fingers skipped over the keys. 'These places always have pictures of their staff. It's a total male vanity, "look at me and just guess how much money I earn" thing. Now here we go. Search for Damien Halliburton.'

His page loaded. And another photograph did indeed accompany a bio short on personal information but long on awards, successes, plaudits from financial magazines, big-name clients and other brokerage houses alike. Both girls sagged a little. He was just the kind of guy who made a woman go weak at the knees.

'He's really dreamy, Chels.'

'Yes, he is,' she admitted.

'Looks fine in a suit.'

'That he does.'

'I'd bet anything he looks just as fine out of it too.'

'And what a pity that you'll never know.'

'So you're meeting at seven o'clock?' Kensey asked.

'That's right,' Chelsea said, biting at a fingernail.

'You'll both be needing dinner about then. How about you casually slip into the conversation something like, "Here's your phone, Damien. And, boy, am I famished? Aren't you famished? Perhaps we could pop inside and unfamish together." Then later, much later, call me. Please. If I don't get a complete rundown on every second I'll never forgive you.'

Kensey kissed her on the cheek, then swanned out of the room. A crash and a bang somewhere else in the building snapped Chelsea completely back to real life. Time she got back to work.

But first... She dialled the number of Amelie's restaurant. It was the kind of place you had to book a month in advance, but she saw no harm in trying. Especially when she had a desk covered in samples of rose-scented doggie shampoos and be-dazzled cat ponchos from which to choose a nice little sweetener for her new favourite cloakroom attendant.

Three o'clock came around slowly. Damien knew as he'd checked his watch a dozen times since he'd found out exactly who had his phone.

He'd probably made less money for his clients that day than he had for himself when his father had insisted he get a job flipping burgers to learn the true value of money, and a hard day's work, during the holidays from his private boys' high school.

Because now he'd decided he was ready to handle some pleasure for pleasure's sake he couldn't think past her voice, her fingers running up and down those gold beads, her lips smiling softly, her crossing her legs and rocking her top foot up and down to some slow, seductive inner rhythm. It was as though she was all he had room for in his mind for.

And the bold truth was he couldn't wait until seven to get a fix.

Needing privacy, especially from Caleb who had an even better radar for sexual tension than for making money, he took a walk into the executive bathroom, checked under the stalls, and, finding himself alone, slid Chelsea's phone from his inside jacket pocket.

Chelsea was in the blue room blow-drying a Persian when the mobile rang. She tugged it from her back pocket, flipped it open, shoved it to her ear and said, 'Chelsea London.'

'Hi,' a by now all too familiar deep male voice said, and she almost dropped the hair-dryer.

'Give me two seconds,' she said, before throwing the phone to the metal bench. She turned off the dryer, put an almost dry Snookums back into her cage, washed her hands, straightened her back, looked in the mirrored wall and flicked a fleck of cat hair from her cheek before picking up the phone again.

'Hi,' she said, her voice breathier than usual.

'How's it going?' Damien asked, the face and the voice merging to create a killer combination.

'Fine,' she said.

'So what are you doing?'

Chelsea frowned. Suddenly she felt as if she were in the eighth grade talking to the boy she'd had a crush on who'd ended up only using her so he could copy off her Biology paper. Another dud to add to the list of men who'd left her disenchanted in the gender as a whole. 'Damien?'

'Yes.'

'Was there something in particular you were after?'

Something about his pause had her holding her breath. The sounds of traffic from nearby Brunswick Street permeated the silence. Until he blew out a fast shot of breath and said, 'I was just thinking about you.'

'Oh,' she said, just managing to make it over to the sunny

window-seat to sit with one leg tucked beneath her. Better that than be upstanding when her knees gave way. 'What were you thinking exactly?'

She could have sworn his voice dropped an octave when he said, 'I was wondering what it is you do for a living.'

And just like that her blood returned to her extremities. He wasn't *thinking* about her as she'd been thinking about him. He was bored. She flicked herself in the side of the head.

'My friend Caleb has a theory that you are in fact a vendor of adult products. I just wanted to set him straight. Or not, if that's the case.'

Chelsea blinked. 'Your friend thought…?'

'He did. He has some imagination, my friend.'

Well, what do you know? she thought. Mr Perfect was nothing at all out of the ordinary. He was just a guy after all.

'Is your friend in the room with you?' she asked, her voice now in total control.

'Not at the moment, no.'

'Well, you can tell him that there is a great way to waste your own time rather than other people's. So why don't you go right ahead and search for me on the Internet.'

And at that she hung up. She threw the phone onto the window-seat where it bounced and settled like a glaring shiny beacon of collective disappointment.

She poked her tongue out at the phone and shot to her feet. But it began to vibrate again. She knew it was him. But she wasn't all that sure what to do with him. Beautiful him. Contradictory him. He was either funny or a jerk. And she wasn't sure which she preferred him to be. Which would give her the chance at a better day's work. A better night's sleep.

With a muffled oath she stormed over and snapped it open. 'Would you prefer I told you to bite me? In case you missed the nuances in my voice that's pretty much what I was trying to say.'

'Chelsea, forgive me,' he said, his voice contrite, and, oh, so deep and delicious she wanted to forgive him. 'It was my attempt at finding a believable reason to call.'

'Why?'

And then he said the only words he could have to redeem himself. 'Because you're the girl who fell into my arms, and spilled my coffee, and stole my phone and gatecrashed my thoughts until I had to admit to her that I've been seriously thinking that a two-minute phone swap isn't what we ought to be doing tonight.'

This time her knees really did give way and she sank back to the window-seat and tucked her spare hand between her knees to stop it from trembling. So much for Damien Halliburton being a mere male clone. She'd never had a man tell her she was *the girl* before.

She closed her eyes shut tight as she said, 'You could have knocked me sideways with a feather when I realised it was you who had my phone too.'

The second the words were out of her mouth she wished she could take them back. She suddenly felt as though the walls around her had been stripped away until she was sitting out in the cold alone. Naked. Unprotected.

She pressed her toes into her shoes, and her shoes into the concrete floor, trying to ground herself. Gambling on a successful business she owned lock, stock and barrel was quite different from gambling with her tender emotions. 'Damien, I—'

He cut her off as though he'd sensed her backtracking. 'So have dinner with me tonight. At Amelie's. I've booked us a table. We can swap phones. Eat. And see where the night takes us from there.'

She opened her eyes, was hit with a burst of bright sunshine from outside. Though the sun hit the cold glass so that she could barely feel its warmth.

Dinner. A date. With the most beautiful man she'd ever met. 'Sure,' she said, wondering where the word even came from. 'Why not?'

'Excellent. So long as you don't mind if we make it a little later. How's nine o'clock?'

'Nine would be fine,' she said, infinitely glad she'd have time to change…either her outfit or her mind. 'Better even. I feel like everything has taken twice as long as normal to be achieved today.'

'All because I have your phone, I suppose,' he suggested, though by the smile in his voice she was sure he knew that wasn't even half the reason. He probably ruined women's concentration spans constantly.

'Of course,' she said smoothly. 'It's all about the phone. So don't forget to bring it at nine.'

'Hmm,' he said, his voice a deep hum that tickled across the back of her neck as certainly as if it were his fingers brushing away her hair. She imagined his lips following. The brief brush of his tongue along the delicate patch of skin… 'And there I was thinking you had some kind of love affair going on with that phone of yours and wanted it back yesterday.'

'I do. I did. I…' She flicked herself again. 'I'll see you at nine, Damien.'

'Until then,' he said, and hung up.

Until then, Chelsea thought, slowly shutting the phone.

She stood and found her reflection in the shiny steel industrial-sized sink in which they washed the cats and miniature dogs and pictured Damien standing behind her, all dark good looks and effortless polish.

She sucked in her stomach and pursed her lips. If you could see past the flat chest and boyish hips, and her slightly crossed front teeth, which had never seen the back end of a pair of braces, her hair was long, her nose passable, and her eyelashes incongruously dark and never in need of mascara.

She let her breath go and slumped into a more normal posture, and her dirt-smudged T-shirt, the third of the day, turned wrinkled and sloppy.

She picked up the closest landline to ring and cancel the seven o'clock table she'd booked, and made a mental note to organise another set of samples for skinny Carrie to keep her mouth shut that the booking had ever existed.

CHAPTER FIVE

BY SEVEN, Damien's employees had all gone home to their wives, husbands and assorted pets while Caleb had a date with an apparently very bendy Cirque de Soleil performer, leaving Damien alone in his big office with only the high winds buffeting his double-glazed window to keep him company.

He checked his watch. Two hours until he was due to meet Chelsea.

He flipped open her phone, pressed the exact right buttons to find her picture and stared at it. Her face half in shadow, half in too-bright light. A shy smile curved her mouth, silky hair tumbled over her shoulders, her pale slender neck seemed to go on for ever.

He ran his thumb back and forth over the image.

She seemed the kind of woman who'd enjoy curling up on a soft, cosy couch on a rainy day, legs tucked beneath a blanket, her head resting on a man's lap, half-empty cups of hot chocolate leaving twin mug rings on the coffee-table while they watched a run of old movies.

He flipped the phone shut with a satisfying snap.

That life would never be his. He was a *Halliburton,* which meant working, living and playing hard. He hadn't spent a day of his life curled up anywhere and he'd never craved hot chocolate.

As he'd blithely walked out her door Bonnie had blamed his parents' divorce for making him as commitment-phobic as he was. He thought it more likely his parents' subsequent friendship without the marriage part getting in the way had more to do with his unwillingness to settle down. Though they had agreed that the sooner he was honest about what exactly he *did* want from any woman who came into his midst, the world would be a safer place. So what the hell was he doing asking a woman like that on a date?

Could it be because he hadn't forgotten the chemical reaction that had lit those golden eyes when she'd first looked into his? The instant surge of attraction. And just like that the image of her on the soft homey couch changed to include a shift of her lithe body, a lifting of her chin as she kissed him, and melted against him, as he spent hours so devoured by her he could no longer remember any other woman he'd ever met.

He ran a hand fast over his face, over his tired eyes, and hard through his hair. So what did he want?

For the rest of his life? He wasn't sure he'd ever be able to answer that question.

But for now, for tonight, he wanted Chelsea. More than he remembered wanting anything in a long time. And until he had a bed of his own, he'd settle for having her wherever he could get her.

It was around a quarter past seven by the time Chelsea made it home.

Home was a beautiful art deco apartment smack bang in the middle of the city. It had been bequeathed to both girls by a maiden aunt on her mother's side, a woman they'd never met or even known had existed since their mother had done a runner in the months after Chelsea herself was born and never been heard from again.

She'd agreed to check the place out unwillingly, but the second she'd set foot inside she'd fallen in love. The chintz lounges, cream panelled walls and curling antique furniture created a warmth and a history the likes of which she'd not known growing up in string of small cold apartments.

Kensey, who at that stage had had a husband, two kids, three chickens and a turtle, had had no need for a one-bedroom city apartment with no yard, so Chelsea had offered to buy her out, convincing herself that prime city real estate was never a gamble.

She now felt great peace in watering the flowers outside her windows, in polishing to a gleam the dining table she never used, and in allowing piles of books and magazines to teeter in corners of the room. Clutter meant permanence, just as dog-loving meant responsibility. Life could be just that simple if one let it.

She kicked off her shoes at the door and aimed for the shower to wash off the day's worth of dog spit, cat hair and other unmentionable ooze.

She padded into the large master bedroom, pulled off her jeans and threw them onto the floor. Her decade-old sweater was halfway over her head when the mobile phone vibrated atop her dresser.

Her heart thumped against her ribs as she screened the call but it wasn't her number looking back at her. It was the offices of Keppler Jones and Morgenstern. It could be important. A message to pass onto Damien in two short hours. Something to fill the conversational void they would no doubt encounter within five minutes of seeing one another again.

She flipped it open. 'Damien Halliburton's phone.'

'Are you still at work?'

Her heart leapt to her throat the instant she heard that sinfully delicious voice.

'Home.' She leant back against the end of the bed for leverage as she pulled off her socks one-handed, and so that he didn't guess she'd come home to change for him she added, 'I had to feed my neighbour's cat. She's away.'

He laughed. 'Caleb knew there'd be a cat somewhere in the picture.'

She wiggled her toes in the lamplight to find at least half of them needed to be re-pinked. 'Caleb's the one who thinks I am a kinky sex-toy purveyor, right?'

'Right.'

She pulled the phone away from her ear briefly to tug her long-sleeved T-shirt over her head. 'Are you sure you shouldn't be finding yourself less troublesome friends?'

'I'm certain I should be. But I'm too nice a guy. Without me he'd be lost.'

'You are Sir Galahad himself.'

'I like to think so.'

Who are you trying to kid? she thought. Conversation with this guy wouldn't be hard to come by. Every topic touched upon seemed to open up between them like a minefield of verbal possibilities.

After a pause he added, 'Are you alone?'

Her undressing came to a sudden halt with her T-shirt hanging off her left shoulder. 'Is that imperative?'

'Not entirely. It would just help clarify my mental picture.'

'You've formed a mental picture?' she asked while flicking the shirt from her arm and through the open door onto the *en suite* floor with the rest of her dirty clothes.

'Haven't you?' he asked.

'Not so much,' she lied.

'Well, just in case you're waiting for me to go first, here's mine.'

He paused for effect. And it worked. Chelsea stood in the centre of her large carpeted bedroom now naked bar a pink lace bra that had seen better days and white cotton knickers, and she held her breath.

'I see an apartment,' he said. 'Lamps everywhere, high ceilings, soft couches a person just sinks into until they never want to get up again. And not an animal print in sight. How am I doing so far?'

Chelsea wrapped an arm around her stomach. 'So far…kind of scary close.'

'Mmm. I'm moving through now, deeper. An ajar door catches my eye. I press it open to find myself in a bedroom. Your bedroom.'

'Just like that? With no invitation? That's pretty forward.'

'Not only am I forward, I'm also not alone.'

'If you tell me there's some snaggle-toothed madman under my bed—'

'Chelsea,' he said with enough force to shut her up.

'Yes, Damien.'

'Did I say you get to talk in my imaginings?'

She shook her head no.

'That's better. Now, I'm not alone in your bedroom because you are there with me. Happy?'

She nodded. And imagined he had just entered, fully dressed in his beautiful suit, one hand in his trouser pocket, pulling his white shirt across his broad chest. His dreamy blue eyes dark in the low light of her muted art deco lamp. She placed the back of her spare hand to her suddenly hot cheek.

'Now, to tell you the truth,' he said, 'I have not one clue what your bedroom looks like. It could be wall-to-wall shag-pile carpeting. It could have bunk beds and beanbags. It could have a disco ball and mirrored ceilings.'

'How disappointing your imagination only stretches so far.'

'Don't be disappointed. All I see right now is you.'

She thanked her lucky stars her bed was there to catch her as she swayed. Permanence and responsibility be damned. She *wanted* him. With a power and a need that ought to have had her hanging up the phone and ordering in. Instead she allowed herself to luxuriate in his smooth, rich, decadent voice.

'What am I wearing?' Chelsea asked, this time dead centre in the middle of his imaginings.

She could all but hear the stretching of his cheeks as his face broke into a sexy smile. 'You tell me.'

Her toes dug into the carpet in order to keep the rest of her upright. Because she knew that this was not just another phone call. This time he had a purpose.

Seduction.

The idea seeped beneath her skin and warmed her cold, tired bones better than the best hot shower in town could ever hope to.

She closed her eyes and reached around behind her to unhook her bra. As it slid over her arms, scraping along her highly sensitised skin, she said, 'I'm naked. Well, not quite.'

His voice was almost unrecognisable when he finally came back with, 'How not quite?'

'Underpants.'

'What kind?'

'Bikini brief.'

'Colour?'

White cotton didn't exactly ring exciting, so she took liberties. 'Burgundy with gold lace.'

Her quivering knees belied her true nerves. She finally gave in and sat on the edge of the bed, crossing her legs to quell the heat already slicing through her centre. 'So what are *you* wearing?'

'I'd love to say I was standing outside your apartment right now wearing nothing bar a bunch of roses and a smile, but unfortunately, unlike you, I *am* still at work.'

'Are *you* alone?'

'As far as I know,' he said.

'So-o-o...'

'So?'

'So it's only fair that if I'm freezing my butt off in nothing bar a tiny sliver of rather flimsy translucent lace that barely covers half my butt cheeks that you do some undressing too.'

The pause was significant as he took the time to add her latest descriptions to his vision. 'But I'm imagining you in your natural environment. Snug in your lovely warm home. Curtains drawn. Locks bolted. Alarm system activated. Killer cat next door to protect you from prying eyes.'

She pumped a coin-sized blob of moisturiser from her bedside table into her palm and began running it up and down her legs, ankle to thigh. The stretch felt good. But it did little to nothing to ease the sexual tension radiating through her. Making her feel wanton. Uncharacteristically reckless.

'Damien,' she purred.

'Yes, Chelsea.'

'I don't think we're playing the same game here.'

'We're not?'

She shook her head, the feel of her hair tumbling down her naked back unbelievably erotic. It was as though every nerve ending were suddenly alight. Every sensation heightened.

She turned and lay down on her stomach, her knees bent, feet in the air rubbing one another. 'My hair is down. My bedroom lights are low and I am naked bar tiny triangles of fabric. And the only way I am getting any more of my kit off is if you do too.'

'Is this really how this is going to go?'

'Things have changed somewhat since Dean Martin ran with a pack. We have equality of the sexes. Or at least wherever we can get it. And two places I insist on it are in the workplace and in the bedroom.'

'How convenient.' This time his pause was momentous. 'You really want me to strip?'

'I really do. Perhaps my imagination isn't quite as good as yours.'

Which was rubbish. She was well and truly in the middle of a great big fantasy about finding a man who craved her so deeply he was willing to get naked, physically and emotionally. And who made her able to feel the same way.

But even now as her feet tingled as they rubbed against one another, as her bare breasts pressed into the quilted comforter, as she kept a man of Damien's calibre on tenterhooks with not much more than a few sharp one-liners, that thread of doubt and mistrust that kept her company on countless lonely nights seeped in beneath the pleasure.

If her upbringing had taught her anything it was that big dreams never really came true. They lingered, they tempted, they dangled just out of reach. What if he was merely setting her up for a one-night stand as he did with every girl whose phone he stole? Normally she'd be able to handle it, but this guy felt…different. He made her feel different. She barely knew him and already she wanted more.

But then Damien Halliburton of the broad shoulders and deep bass voice said, 'Fine,' followed by the sound of his phone hitting wood with a thunk.

She pressed her phone to her ear to better hear a rustle of

cotton, the slide of satin lining, and the distinct whir of a zipper, and felt as though everything she'd ever believed about men like Damien, who'd so obviously had advantages and experiences she could never dream of, was slowly but surely turning on its head.

'Right,' he said a few moments later, his voice a tad breathless. 'I'm down to my jocks.'

A bubble of laughter gurgled up into her throat and out her mouth.

'Are you laughing at me now?' he asked.

'No. Not really. I…' By now the bubble had burst and she was really laughing, lying back on her bed with her legs dangling over the side, holding her stomach. 'I'm just picturing you in some great hulking swanky up-town office with the city sprawled out dark and twinkly behind you, and you in Y-fronts, brown socks and black shoes.'

His pause spoke volumes. As did the clunk, clunk, that accompanied his shoes as he kicked them off.

'My socks are black, thank you very much.'

'Well, then, either you have a very involved mother or a woman organises your sock drawer.'

His voice was dry as he said, 'I haven't worn brown socks since grade school.'

'Meaning no interfering mother or girlfriend to speak of?' she asked, then she bit her lip and scrunched up her eyes.

'My mother is too busy interfering in my father's life to worry about mine,' he said. 'And no. No girlfriend.'

She let out a breath she didn't even know she'd been holding.

'You?' he asked.

She shook her head. 'No mother. No girlfriend.'

'Funny. I've found myself a funny girl. Tell me there is no man in your life whose sock drawer you organise on a regular basis.'

His demand was so serious the tension coursing through her slid away until she rolled over and let her spare arm flail sideways. Loose. Warm. Limber.

'No man,' she said. 'Not a single one.'

'Good to know.'

This was getting ridiculous. She was practically naked, and lolling about on her bed as if she were a teenager, hoping the boy she had a crush on might like her back. But this was no boy. This was a grown man with the knowledge and confidence that came with being an honest to goodness walking aphrodisiac.

'So are you wearing Y-fronts?' Her voice was little higher than a vibration.

'Boxers.'

'Cotton?'

'Silk.'

'Colour?'

'Black.' Then after a pause, 'With little pictures of ducks all over them.'

Chelsea laughed again, amazed that he was being truly honest. Amazed and a little taken aback. While she was in the middle of a 'close your eyes and think of goose-down pillows, king-sized sheets, and the first touch of a beautiful stranger' fantasy, everything he had said and done so far pointed to the fact that he was utterly present.

She rolled over and sat up, crossing her legs and biting at her fingernail. Unless...

'Take a photo,' she demanded.

'Excuse me?'

'I don't believe you're not sitting there in your big plush office unzipping pencil cases and tapping pencils on your desk to sound like buttons popping.'

'Now what have I done to make it so hard for you to trust me so quickly?'

'Don't take it personally. I don't trust anybody. I want proof.'

'Fine. Ditto,' he shot back.

Okay, so that had backfired. 'I'm not sending you a picture of me half naked!'

'No trust. So sad. Yet you desperately want a naked picture of me. Interesting.'

'Not *interesting,* I just don't want a photo of me to end up on some Internet porn site where my sister's kids can find it.'

'They are allowed to browse porn sites? That's some forward-thinking sister you have there. Maybe I want her phone number instead.'

'Don't be ridiculous,' she said. 'And she's married. Happily. And pregnant.'

And would die laughing if she knew her intractable little sister was on the verge of engaging in phone sex with the hottest man on the planet, yet finding myriad modes of sabotaging it every step of the way.

'But you know how kids are.'

'Actually, I don't.'

'No nieces or nephews?'

'Nope. One sister, Ava. Perennial student. Studying at Harvard this year. Not the lay-down-your-hat kind at all. Therefore no kids.'

'That's a pity. They're a riot.'

'And sneaky, so it seems.'

It hit her then that somehow she'd found out more about this guy in one phone call than she had about her last three dates collectively. She wondered just how much she'd inadvertently given away in turn.

'Now, tell me,' he said, 'did you turn the conversation

because you are trying to avoid me seeing you half naked? Or is there something else you're trying to avoid?'

How did he know? 'Maybe I'm just not in the mood any more.'

'Meaning you were?'

'Meaning…I'm not sure.'

'About what exactly?'

'This.'

'And what is this?'

'I don't know. You rang me. You tell me what this is.'

Again the pause. Which was the one thing she hated about having spent so much time on the phone with the guy while she found herself getting deeper and deeper into some potent, totally crazy, out-of-control attraction towards him: she never got to see his expression, the look in his eyes, to know the nuances of his voice. If she'd read him wrong from the beginning…

But then he once again pulled the perfect words from thin air, saying, 'This was meant to be me finding a way to be with you again as soon as I possibly could.'

'You'll see me in two hours.'

'I couldn't wait two hours.'

That one deserved a gulp. If he was straining that badly at the bit she was kind of terrified about what might happen when they did meet; terrified that the sparks would make them both combust on the spot and equally afraid they wouldn't.

She'd never been this messed up about seeing a man before. But he made her feel as if the world were rushing so fast beneath her feet it was passing by in a blur. She needed to get her feet on solid ground again.

'Damien—' she began.

'Chelsea,' he warned, cutting her off. 'I want you to know

that I'm normally extremely content with the headlong daily routine that makes up my life. But from the moment you landed in my arms…' He took a breath that could have come from her own over-taut lungs. 'Let's say I've ended up standing still in my office in my boxer shorts and I'm beginning to notice there is a draught.'

'So get dressed,' was the only thing she could think to say.

'I plan to. But I also need for you to make me one small promise.'

She dug her hand into a fist, biting into the back of her thigh. 'Okay…'

'I'll get dressed if you promise me you won't.'

'Ever?'

He laughed. She liquefied.

'Not for the next hour,' he said.

'So your imagination doesn't stretch as far as you thought it did.'

'My imagination stretches plenty far, and I want you to slide off that bikini brief, throw it over your shoulder with no care as to where it lands, then I want you to lie back on that large soft bed of yours and let me show you just how far my imagination can take you.'

CHAPTER SIX

'LIE back,' Damien insisted.

'Come over,' Chelsea said, rashness searing her veins and making all sense flee. 'Let's forget Amelie's.'

'Ain't gonna happen.'

Hot, then cold. He was driving her crazy. Making her reckless. Making her want to try harder, gamble more, do whatever it took to get what she wanted, which was to release this agonising pressure that had her pinned, half naked, to her bed.

'Now do as you're told, and lie back. Make yourself comfortable.'

She wanted to. More than almost anything she could remember wanting in her life she wanted to give in to the firmness in his deep voice. But the yearning to have him there beside her, to watch his eyes turn dark with pleasure, pulsed through her like a drug. An addiction. 'You are driving me crazy, Damien.'

'Welcome to the club.'

'So why won't you come over here and do something about it that will satisfy the both of us?'

If it's to be a one-night stand, she thought, *then let it be that.*

'Because that's not *all* I want from you.'

It wasn't?

'What else can you possibly want?' she asked, her voice weak as a kitten.

'I want dinner. I want conversation. I want to watch you over the top of a stubby candle, a couple of wineglasses and a half-finished steak.'

'Can't you use that renowned imagination of yours to imagine that part instead?'

He laughed, the sound warming the various minuscule bits of her that weren't already burning hot. 'Are you trying to make my unusually gentlemanly behaviour even more difficult?'

'Well, yes, actually.'

He laughed again. And since her skin was saturated with sensation, this time she felt it deeper inside. Just behind her ribs and a little to the left. She pressed her hand to the spot as though needing to check it was really real.

'You, Chelsea London, are some woman.'

'I've always thought so.'

'Which is why I am putting my clothes back on right now, and hanging up and not calling you again before nine regardless of how much I might want to. Unless...'

'Unless I let you seduce me over the phone line.'

'Mmm.'

His murmur was almost enough to put her over the edge into acquiescence. But not quite. She knew in her heart of hearts it would be far more sensible to talk to him face to face over the top of a stubby candle before she let him into her bed, or any deeper under her skin.

Chelsea grabbed an angora throw rug from the end of the bed and wrapped it around herself as though it would somehow make her seem more demure, less like the raging sexpot she had been a minute before. 'So nine o'clock?'

'Outside Amelie's,' he said. 'I'll be the one with the rose in my lapel.'

'I thought we'd already agreed that was the mark of a date.'

'So we did.'

'So this is a date?'

Again the pause, and again she wished she could see the look in his eyes to know what it meant.

'So it seems,' he finally said. 'See you soon, Chelsea.'

'Bye.' She hung up. Slowly. And let the warm phone rest against her lips for a few moments as her heart rate slowed, and her nerve endings stopped overreacting to every sound, thought and movement.

She glanced at the other side of the bed. Empty, pillow long since undisturbed by a friendly head. And her heart twisted.

'Careful,' she warned herself out loud.

Damien hung up the mobile phone and slowly pulled his clothes back on realising he had actually turned Chelsea down.

The second she'd offered he should have been over there in a flash. God knew he'd be kicking himself ten ways from Sunday as he railed against peak-hour traffic while driving back to Caleb's.

He'd convinced himself it was all he wanted. But as it turned out he could wait. He was a sophisticated man, not some creature controlled by nothing but his basest needs. He wasn't Caleb.

As he fixed the knot of his tie he stared at the sleek black and silver contraption lying, oh, so innocently on his large desk. 'Hold me. Use me,' it called to his subconscious.

But some other part of him spoke louder. His instincts told him that ravaging Chelsea senseless might well give him some relief, but he had no idea how it would affect her. And after how effortlessly he'd hurt Bonnie he had to keep that in mind if he was ever to look himself in the mirror again.

He could back up a step. He could sit down to dinner with Chelsea. And in doing so he could test the waters more thoroughly to see if a wild night wrapped in her lean limbs was still on the cards.

The very thought had him jerk his tie knot until it almost strangled him. He eased it back, then shut down his computer and, seeing his reflection in the dark blank screen, said, 'Just be careful.'

At nine that evening Chelsea stood outside Amelie's, her gloved hands holding her old pink tartan coat tighter about her body.

The footpath was bustling as the weather was as good as could be expected for a Melbourne autumn night: breezy cool, starlit, yet giving people ideas about getting indoors and getting warm however they could.

An extra several layers beneath instead of her chocolate crossover wool dress would have been more sensible. But at least it didn't smell of mothballs, and it was the most date-worthy thing she owned.

She rubbed her arms as she scoured the crowd while trying not to look as eager as she felt.

Damien stood at the end of the block, hands deep in his trouser pockets. His eyes were zeroed in on the slender caramel-blonde struggling with her coat, her fly-away hair, and the jostling crowd outside Amelie's.

Again she was like a burst of sunshine amidst the river of Melbourne black. And again she infused him with as much energy as though she'd hit him with a stun gun.

A gust of wind whipped down the street, ruffling his hair. It whipped her glittery gold scarf from around her neck, sending it fluttering to the ground with the grace of an autumn leaf. She forgot her coat, which split open as she leant over to pick up her scarf revealing a glimpse of lean honey-golden leg curving in and out in all the right places and feminine curves poured into some stretchy brown fabric that hid just enough and hinted at everything.

Her dress tipped forward and Damien saw a hint of bra. Pale pink. Half cup. He could barely suppress his groan.

She stood, wrapped herself up tight and looked at her watch and he took it as a sign that he'd better get a move on. He cleared his throat, ran a quick hand through his hair, checked his breath on his palm and headed down the street towards the hopeful release of a month's worth of holding back from what no man should rightfully have to forfeit if he could possibly help it.

Chelsea watched as the fiftieth dark suit in eight minutes rounded the corner.

But this one was a half-head taller. A couple of inches broader. Dark hair gleamed under the lamplight. And the length of his strides meant that people simply got out of his way. She wasn't sure it was Damien, but at the same time she just knew that it was.

He neared. He was even more beautiful than she remembered. More blessed by the gods of all things extraordinary. Through the noisy crowd their eyes caught and held. *Pacific-blue,* she thought with an internal sigh, *like the ocean at night.*

'Hi, Damien,' she said.

'Chelsea,' he said as he stopped in front of her.

She must have swayed towards him, or maybe it was an optical illusion, but he suddenly felt closer. And then he was leaning in towards her. She instinctively lifted her cheek for a friendly peck, but instead his lips landed square upon hers. She blinked in shock for a good second or two before his mouth began to move over hers.

As her eyes flittered closed her hand fluttered up to land gently upon his chest. His arm slunk around her back to pull her closer. And right there, in front of a street full of bustling pedestrians, everything floated away, leaving only the taste of him, the scent of him, the feel of his heavenly lips. Her hand curled into his shirt, and she hoped against hope that would be enough to keep her from collapsing in a puddle at his feet.

When the kiss broke her eyes opened. A small smile lit his, creases fanning out from the edges.

'Well, what do you know?' he said, his voice low, rumbling, pure sensuality.

Needing to catch her breath and regather her scattered senses, she slid her hand away and put a metre of space between them. Then she pulled his phone out of her clutch purse and held it out for him on an upturned palm.

'Right,' he said, closing his eyes and shaking his head as though he'd completely forgotten why they were really there. He opened his jacket, once again revealing a broad mass of starched white shirt and enveloping her in a wave of his light but wholly masculine scent. She breathed deep.

He found her phone and held it out to her. Her left palm tickled as he slid his gently from her grasp, while her right hand immediately soaked in the warmth still remaining in the phone she now had back.

'So,' Damien said. 'Now that the formalities are out of the way, shall we?'

Formalities? Kissing her to the point of melting her knees from the inside out was to him a *formality?* Boy, oh, boy. What was she letting herself in for?

He held out an elbow. She tugged her hand into a tight ball to get the feeling back before placing it in the crook of his arm. He tucked her tight against him, drawing her close enough so that the heavy pedestrian traffic could not break their hold, and so that she could again smell the scent of autumn clinging to his clothes.

During the day the restaurant had been bright and bustling, all flashy money and flashier people checking to see who was walking through the front doors.

But at night it was as if they had walked into a cave. It was warm and dark, the ceiling lights recessed so that the whole place seemed lit only by discreetly scattered candles bathing it in a dark red light. It was so romantic. More than romantic. Decadent. As if an orgy could break out at any second.

Damien pressed a gentle hand to Chelsea's back and she jumped. She could feel the heat of his palm searing through the heavy coat and straight to her skin. He leaned forward to whisper against her ear. 'I think she wants our phones.'

Her gaze shot to the hostess. Tall, skinny, brunette hair to her waist and staring at Damien with a small smile and her hand outstretched as though she'd take from him whatever he chose to give her.

Chelsea glanced back at Damien to find herself so close to him she could see just how close he'd shaved before coming to meet her tonight. It somehow gave her a jolt of confidence.

'Do you think we should revolt?' she asked as she slid her coat and scarf from her back.

'I haven't eaten since lunch,' he growled. 'I'm starving.'

She glanced back again to find his gaze had been inexorably drawn to the neckline of her dress. To the barely there hint of cleavage deep within the V. His eyes slid up to hers, connected. Actually, it was more as if they clashed, sending little sparks of heat all over her body.

Chelsea handed over her phone and coat and said, 'I give in.'

'That's my girl,' Damien said, and handed his phone to the hostess. 'In the same compartment, if you please. These two have a way of causing trouble if left on their own.'

The woman's smile faltered as she realised she was beaten before she'd even had the chance to play.

And while Chelsea watched the phones with an eagle eye, she sensed that Damien didn't once take his eyes off her as he waited for the numbered ticket to be placed into his outstretched hand. He slid the ticket inside his jacket pocket, and she realised that she wouldn't be leaving the restaurant without him unless she wanted to leave her phone behind too.

'Where would you be comfortable sitting?' the waitress asked as she picked up a couple of menus.

'I think it's far too late for all that,' Damien said beneath his breath, but Chelsea heard him loud and clear.

She'd had crushes before, but for the first time in her whole life she was absolutely in lust. He created in her urgency that beat down every other wholly sensible qualm. She hung on to her clutch purse with both hands to stop herself from taking him by the hand and dragging him to the nearest dark alley. Hard bodies, slick, sweaty limbs, and nothing left the next morning bar the lingering scent of day-old aftershave.

Damien breathed out hard before turning back to the brunette and Chelsea thankfully felt the hook through her chest melt away.

'A nice private corner would suit us well,' Damien said. He smiled, the low light doing things to his eyes that made her stomach turn to liquid.

'No problem,' the hostess said. 'Follow me.'

Damien held out an arm to encourage Chelsea to go first. What he really wanted to do was continue where they'd left off outside, to lean in, slide his hand around her waist, and kiss the point where her neck met her shoulder, but instead he placed a gentlemanly hand in the small of her back and followed.

Beneath the soft fabric of her dress her skin was warm. Tugging left then right with each swaying step. He closed his eyes for a second and begged heaven to help him make it through dinner without giving in to the desire swarming over him.

They reached the private booth in a far dark corner of the room. Before the hostess had the chance he pulled the table away from the wall so that Chelsea had to slide past him to get to her seat.

He was breathing perfectly normally up until that point. Until he swallowed a mouthful of her scent. Sweet, airy, gentle; the complete antithesis of the sensual vision before him.

The woman was a walking dichotomy. It only made him want her more yet in the same breath made him fear she was exactly the wrong girl for the job.

'Much appreciated,' Chelsea said, smiling up at him from beneath her lashes.

Damien slid behind the table at a right angle to her, and allowed the hostess to lock them into place, glad to have a table hiding his lap.

'Any drinks for starters?' the brunette asked.

'God, yes,' Chelsea shot out at the same time that Damien said,

'I asked for a bottle of Mount Mary Pinot Noir 1993 to be placed on hold under Halliburton.'

'Oh,' the brunette said, her eyes widening. Then she collected herself, nodded, and sent Damien one last lingering look that should have made him puff out his chest even though he was in the company of another woman. But she left him completely unaffected.

Then he and Chelsea were alone, hidden from view of the rest of the restaurant by the angle of their table, a large potted Ficus and the clever lighting. Their booth was cramped. But intimate. Low candlelight flickering from an alcove on the rendered wall above shot waves of gold through Chelsea's hair, and created shadows beneath her lashes, her nose, and full lower lip.

Simply looking at her, he felt anything but unaffected.

A waiter with an eyebrow ring and three more through his nose came back with their wine. Damien did the whole sniff, sip, thumbs up before they were each poured a healthy glass and the bottle was left in an icebox nearby.

Chelsea fussed with her dress, her hair, the placement of the napkin in front of her and said, 'There is something I've been meaning to ask you.'

Damien leant his elbow on the table and his chin on his palm. 'This should be good.'

Her hands fluttered to her lap, but she gave him direct eye contact. All golden light and sunshine and radiant energy. He could have snuffed out the candle and his senses would have told him exactly where she sat.

She asked, 'Whatever did happen to Keppler-Jones and Whosiwhatsit?'

The laughter that burst from Damien's chest was so sudden he almost pulled a muscle. He leant back in his chair and rubbed the strange spot of discomfort beneath his left pec. 'Meaning did I knock them off in order to get a corner office?'

She took a sip of her wine, smiling at him from over the glass. 'Your words, not mine.'

He leaned forward again. 'You have to promise me that this will go no further.'

'Cross my heart,' she said, and the action tugged his gaze to her chest where the stretch fabric clung to her curves.

He licked his lips before dragging his eyes north and saying, 'It was a dark and stormy night.'

Her eyes gleamed. 'Isn't it always?'

'The company had been around since long before the heydays of the eighties. Jones was a family friend of my god-father and I worked for them part-time while studying business/law at university and stayed on afterward. Once I'd risen as far in the firm as a non-partner could I made them an offer they couldn't refuse.'

'And the dark and stormy night?'

'Was the retirement party. One to go down in the history books. I'm certain it took five years off each of their lives. That's my story and I'm sticking to it. Now tell me about the animal-print dog-collar connection before I go any further into imagining what kind of job would make you some kind of expert fit for *Chic* magazine.'

She grinned up at him. He could practically feel the blood in his veins revving itself up to explode through his system the second talking finally turned to touching. And before the end of this night there *would* be touching.

'I own and run a pet-grooming salon in Fitzroy. Disappointed?'

'Infinitely,' he said with an answering smile. 'So what was it about clipping dog toenails that drew you to the cause?'

She shook her hair off her shoulders and sat back in her chair, into deeper shadow, her face in richer relief. 'There's a tad more to what I do than clipping dog toenails.'

'Surprise me.'

'We see up to sixty clients a day. Their treatments can include brushing, dematting, therapeutic baths, fluff or towel dry, nail-clipping, haircuts and shave-downs. They leave us looking brand-new. *Feeling* brand-new.'

'And don't we all need to feel that way every now and then?' he said.

Her glorious eyes shone with a fire that was pure dynamite. He couldn't remember feeling lit by such an inner blaze. It had him wondering if his life was far too comfortable. Maybe it could do with a little spicing up.

'Come on down one day,' she said, 'and I'll give you the works. I'll guarantee you'd leave the place unrecognisable. And flea-free.'

Damien laughed, though truth be told his mind hadn't gone much further than *the works*. Imagining those small hands giving him a therapeutic bath and a towel dry was almost his undoing.

'It's some kind of thrill, don't you think?' he asked.

Her right eyebrow rose in question.

'Working for oneself. Balancing the kind of satisfaction, control and wealth you can only gain if you own the business against the daily possibility of losing everything. I like to think of it as a masochistic gamble rather than anything as mundane as a job.'

She again reached for her wine. 'Unless you never gamble more than you can afford to lose.'

'Never?'

She shook her head.

'Then that's not really a gamble at all, is it?'

She shook her head again, a small smile lifting the corners of her mouth as though she knew some great secret he and the rest of the world had yet to catch onto.

'That said,' she added, 'I had a meeting with the bank today and they have approved a loan for me to expand out to three salons.'

'Good for you. It seems this is a celebratory dinner as well.' He topped her up wine.

She watched as the dark liquid poured into her deep glass,

then said, 'But I'm not sure if I want to sign.' She added a little shrug, then sank further away from him again as though she'd said more than she'd meant to.

'Why not?' he asked, adding a dash to his own mostly full glass. 'If they think you warrant such an investment, they have faith in your product.'

'I guess. But I'm not sure that I'm willing to put all my faith in someone else's judgment.'

For the first time Damien *saw* the genuine vulnerability he'd sensed all along in the lift of her cheek, the blush across her neck, the shy tilt of her head.

He shifted in his seat, mighty glad he hadn't zoomed over to her place as she'd begged him to do. Right about now he'd be dealing with the fallout. With those great golden eyes boring holes in his back as he walked out of her life as he was wont to do. He thanked his lucky stars he hadn't gone so far he didn't still have time to pull out graciously without hurting her feelings.

'Am I being ridiculous?' she asked.

It took him a moment to remember what they were talking about. He gulped down half his wine before saying, 'If your bank works anything like my team do, they keep their ears to the ground. We watch the news, read the papers, I even have a team on gossip magazines, as you never know where new market patterns will emerge.'

'But once you see something worth your attention you know it? It's that simple for you?'

'It really is. And then I gamble everything at my disposal on that instinct.'

'What if your instincts are wrong?'

'What if they're not?'

She looked up at him from beneath the shadow of her long

lashes. Her lower lip disappeared between her teeth. And he knew there was far more going on behind the golden depths of her eyes than the conversation at hand. It seemed he wasn't the only one ignoring the elephant in the room—an attraction so intense he wasn't sure just how long he and his chivalry could hold out.

'So now that I've given you some free financial advice,' he said, 'you owe me.' He turned over his palm and pulled a pretend pen from behind his ear. 'Give me the address of your business. It's time I had a haircut.'

At that she laughed, as he'd hoped she might; only the footloose sound stirred all sorts of shackled feelings deep inside him, enough for him to keep on pouring until his wineglass was full all the way to the top.

CHAPTER SEVEN

CHELSEA kicked off her shoes beneath the table and rubbed life back into the balls of her feet.

She wanted nothing more than to run her bare foot up the inside of Damien's trousers. To scrape her toenails along a length of manly leg hair and just forget all about dinner. He was so utterly and totally beyond the realms of gorgeous that her nerve endings felt as if they were on constant red alert.

Added to that she was beginning to *like* him. To really, actually like the guy. Beneath the suit and tie he was nice. Funny. Sharp. Thoughtful. And he kept looking at her as if he wanted nothing more than to continue the kiss he'd started outside.

But, and it was a huge but, it seemed he was that mythical creature that she had spent her whole life both desperately wishing to know really existed, while at the same time despising to the depths of her soul.

He was a gambler. Who won. And again and again by the looks of him. By the loose way he sat in the chair. The ease with which he wore his immaculate clothes. The way he rattled off the name of some no doubt ridiculously expensive bottle of wine.

And for him to always win meant guys like her dad had to always lose.

She grabbed the leftover cork from the wine bottle and spun it over her knuckles, from one end of her hand to the other with ever increasing speed.

There was only one way to settle this. The clincher that she had always known since she was a little girl must determine the worthwhile men from the jerks.

'Do you have a dog?' she asked.

He looked up from his perusal of the dinner menu. 'Ah, no.'

There is no point in liking him. Unless, perhaps, the question merely needs one more qualifier. 'Do you *like* dogs?'

'I love dogs. I had a golden lab when I was a kid. Buster. He had an inner-ear problem and ran into walls all the time.'

'He did no such thing.'

'You have no idea. He was the best sounding-board a boy could have. Helped me get over my father's wrath when I got a C in history. He helped me get over being dumped by Casey Campanalli in the eight grade. Helped me survive my parents' trigger-happy divorce. To this day he's still the best hug I've ever had.'

Chelsea bit her cheek to stop from sighing. He was born to wear a suit. He was born to eat in expensive restaurants day in and day out. He had a natural reserve about him that had her instincts screaming at her to back away fast. But Damien Halliburton was a *true* dog lover.

The plumber had wanted a dog for company. The single dad had been landed with his in the divorce. The consultant had treated his dogs as if they were his children. But this guy…he had understood the importance of having love in your life that was not for sale.

She *liked* the guy. She *wanted* him. And now he'd accidentally made contact with the deepest personal touchstone she had in her arsenal. She was in trouble.

She flicked the cork into her palm, then onto the back of her hand, then continued twirling it over her knuckles. 'So yours wasn't an idyllic childhood, then?'

'I have no complaints. Both parents are still well and truly around and I do believe, on their diet of matching dirty martinis and tennis three times a week, they will live for ever. They divorced when I was eleven, which is likely why they are on such good terms and are now the poster children for contented singledom.'

He smiled, as much as spelling out to her that he was happy being single too. Which was great. So was she. Single and in charge of her own destiny. So why did it feel as if her stomach had sunk like a stone?

Damien took a sip of wine and watched her over the top of the glass, his deep blue eyes smiling, seeing. His mouth stretched into a smile that was built to make a woman just want to give in and surrender. 'You like me more now, don't you?'

She leant her chin on her upturned palm, stared right on back and called his bluff. 'Infinitely.'

His eyes narrowed as he watched her for several more seconds before shifting in his chair, stretching out his legs. The air around her knees wafted and her skirt blew up before settling back against her suddenly sensitive skin.

'So do you have a dog?' he asked.

'I live in an apartment. I'm out a lot. It wouldn't be fair.'

He nodded. And she restlessly spun the rounded end of the cork on the end of her pointer finger before it landed on the back of her hand again.

'Okay, I bite,' Damien said, his dark gaze dropping to her hands. 'Either you were once a croupier in some dive in Vegas or…nope, that's the only thing I can come up with for a girl with that kind of hand-eye coordination. Give me a go.'

She tossed it in the air so it spun, and by the time he'd caught it she sat back swirling his wineglass in her left hand and hers in her right.

His eyes grew wide. And impressed. They slid up her chest, past her neck, warming every inch of exposed skin along the way until they landed with a heated thud on her eyes. 'You're some kind of witch, aren't you?'

Laughter tickled her throat. 'And I'd gone to so much trouble to hide my broomstick out of sight in an alley down the street.'

Only after taking a decided sip from his glass did she give him back his wine.

'Thank you,' he said with a new kind of smile in his eyes that did violent things to her heart rate.

'My pleasure.'

He threw the cork in the air, then spent a good thirty seconds trying to flip it across his knuckles but he only succeeded in dropping it again and again. 'Where *did* you learn to do that?'

She grabbed the linen napkin and began folding it into smaller and smaller triangles, using it as an excuse to break eye contact. She thought about lying. She'd certainly done it before: hidden her own inadequacies while frenetically determining those of any otherwise likeable man in her midst.

She sat back in her chair and pretended to be on the lookout for a waiter. 'Why is it always the posh places that give such slow service?'

'Chelsea, spill. Or I'll find a way to make you.'

She blinked back at him. This guy… Something made her want to tell the truth. Hoping it would bring them closer, or push him further away?

'My father was a grifter.'

'Like a conman?'

She tucked a strand of hair behind her ear. 'Every once in a while. But more consistently a gambler, always following the next big dream, looking for the next sure thing which would make us rich. And when that failed, as it inevitably did, he would turn to stealing wallets, identities, candy from babies as he moved us from pillar to post and back again.'

She glanced at Damien and away again to give herself enough time to see if he was looking for the nearest exit. If she were in his shoes that was what she would have been doing. But if anything he was sitting further forward, intrigue adding a further glint to his eyes. No matter which way she thought he'd spin he continued to surprise her.

She took a much needed deep breath and crossed her feet at the ankles, accidentally brushing the side of her bare foot against his calf. She stilled, wondering if he'd even noticed. When his eyes grew a shade darker and he took his own deep breath she knew he'd noticed all right. Noticed and reacted instantly.

He lounged a tad more, shifting until his knees came so close to hers she could feel his warmth against her bare skin. And that time she just knew it wasn't in the least bit accidental.

'So could you steal my wallet?' he asked.

Chelsea glanced at the region of his heart where by habit she'd felt the consistency of a flat leather wallet that first day. 'What makes you think I haven't already?'

His eyes grew wide as his hand flew to the spot. He slid his long black leather wallet from its home and let out a long slow breath. Then his eyes shot to hers. Flickered left to right. Dark, searching, mesmerised.

He slid his wallet back into place, his eyes not leaving hers. Their depths glinted as though reflecting the last gasp of sunlight of the day.

Her teeth scraped against the edge of her glass. The zing she felt through her jaw at the clash of hard substances was nothing compared with the zing singing through her stomach, ricocheting from surface to surface until she felt as if a truckload of fireworks had gone off inside her belly.

'I'm not sure whether to find you a complete delight or to fear what each encounter with you will bring, Miss London.'

He reached for his own glass of wine, but merely swirled it beneath his chin as his gaze roamed lazily over her face, her hair, and her breasts, which strained against the tight fabric of her dress as though he'd actually reached out and grazed them with his touch.

Finally he looked back into her eyes. A smile warming them. Warming her. Challenging her.

He said, 'Right now I'm leaning heavily towards delight.'

Chelsea pressed her knees together. She was the one who ought to be feeling fearful of what each meeting with this man might bring. She who was usually so untouchable was becoming very very touched. And the need to touch and be touched as long as she could handle it was overwhelming. She fought to find a way to relieve the pressure inside her before it exploded into something terribly messy like genuine affection.

'Your turn,' she said.

'For?'

'A party trick. It's another family tradition of mine. On the rare occasions we ate out anywhere fancy Kensey and I would always end up trying to outdo one another by performing the strangest acts we could while not drawing attention to ourselves. For example...' She crossed her eyes and curled her tongue into a tube.

Sabotage, her sister would have called it. Chelsea liked to think it was better to know the measure of a man as soon as possible. When she uncrossed them Damien was still watching her with such a look of honest fascination she had to scrape her tongue back through her teeth to stop the tingling.

'I have something you might like.' His voice had dropped low and deep. Enough for the sound to create skitters of awareness across her arms. 'We have to go uncaught? That's the rule?'

Chelsea's feet and hands cooled as all the blood inside her seemed to rush to her cheeks. To the vertical dip between her breasts. And lower.

She nodded.

'Right. Then I'm going to need a drink.' He turned his wineglass so that the exact spot from which she had earlier drunk was facing him. He brought it to his lips and took a sip, letting his mouth rest around the lip of the glass a mite longer than entirely necessary.

Her lips tingled as though his were pressed just as surely and closely against her own. His breath tickling her tongue rather than creating minuscule waves in his glass.

The upholstered booth seat beneath her suddenly felt as though it were tipping. And when he unbuttoned his jacket, and loosened his tie, then dropped his hands beneath the table and leant forward so that she could see the splash of navy surrounding each of his ocean-blue eyes she clung onto the edge of the table to stop herself from swaying under his gaze.

'Ready?' he asked.

'Am I meant to be involved in this somehow?'

'Mmm, that's the general plan.'

'What do I need to do?'

'Keep very very still. And if you give us away then you lose, and I win, right?'

She nodded.

And in the next instant the back of his knuckles grazed gently across her knees.

Chelsea's bare toes dug into the carpeted floor. Her fingers gripped the table so hard her knuckles were turning white. 'What is it exactly that you are thinking of doing?'

'Believe me when I say this game will be that much more fun if we left that a surprise.'

When she didn't flinch, or protest, the knuckles made a return journey, this time brushing across her knees and around the outside until his thumbs ran over the top of her kneecaps and just beneath the hem of her skirt. And she kept her mouth shut tight.

When he touched her for a third time Chelsea glanced quickly around the restaurant, but it was dark, and the table positioned just so. Unless someone came leaping out from behind the Ficus…

Damien's thumb ran back and forth beneath her skirt and she drew in a shuddering breath. And when his hands wrapped around the outside of her thighs and began sliding up her legs, she wasn't sure when she ever might find the chance to breathe again.

He smiled. Though it was more of a tilt of the lips, a deepening of the creases below his cheeks, and a change in the colour of his eyes. But in that smile she saw arrogance, confidence, and purpose. Damien Halliburton knew just what kind of power he had over her.

Her head protested. But it was too late. Nothing could have prepared her for the mass of sensation that spread like wildfire through her whole body when his hands slid over the tops of her thighs, his thumbs delved into the gap between and gently, but insistently, pressed her legs apart.

She let her eyes flutter closed. He was so supremely sure of his effect on her, while the only times in recent history she'd had a male get this close was when she'd had to straddle the Kellets' Great Dane to hold it in place while Phyllis clipped its nails.

She squeezed her eyes tighter. *That's it, you idiot,* she said to herself. *You are in the middle of the sexiest moment of your entire life and you are doing your best to diminish it. To distance yourself. Well, not this time.*

This time it felt too good. This time it had been building and building and unless she let it come to its natural conclusion she knew she would never forgive herself. This time she slowly uncrossed her ankles, released her death grip on the table and let the pressure of his thumbs guide her knees inches apart.

Her pulse pounded beneath her skin, which felt so hot it almost hurt to move. Her head suddenly felt loose upon her neck. And a trickle of perspiration made a slow, hot trail down her spine.

Ambient sounds of the restaurant served as a cushion to her senses: the soft murmur of voices, the whisper of footsteps on expensive carpet, the chime of cutlery against dinner plates. And above it all, like a pulse throbbing across her skin, were Damien's deep intakes and slow releases of breath, evidence that beneath his self-assurance he was as affected as she was.

He twisted his hands until his fingers were splayed atop her thighs. He tightened his grip, digging into the tense muscle for a brief second before his left hand disappeared. She almost cried out for the sudden erasure of half her pleasure.

Until his right hand continued its journey, circling her thigh until it dived between the two. Her legs spasmed. Clutching at his hand. But it wasn't to be deterred. The backs of his knuckles grazed one inner thigh, while the pads of his fingers dug into the soft flesh of the other. Then slowed imperceptibly until he came to a stop at the edge of her cotton briefs.

'Chelsea,' he said, his deep voice seeming to come to her from a mile away.

'Yes,' she managed to breathe out. *Yes, yes, yes!*

'Is this the kind of thing you had in mind?' His fingers teased at the edge of her panties, brushing ever so lightly around the hem. *Since the moment I laid eyes on you,* she thought.

She began to tremble. Her hands shot to grip onto the padded bench. Her toes dug harder into the soft carpet. Her tongue darted out to wet her lips, which felt as if they were burning up. 'So far so good.'

He laughed, the sound vibrating through his arm and into his hand. Until her legs eased further apart. Just enough to give him all the access he desired.

Then, with no more finessing, one finger slipped behind the cotton barrier, then two. And her whole body shook with such a tremendous release of tension; hours' worth, weeks, years, a lifetime worth of holding everything close to her chest lest someone take what little she had away from her.

This trick, this *game,* was no longer anything of the sort. As with her eyes closed tight, her knees shoulder-width apart, and her usual abundance of common sense having taken leave on another planet, she put every ounce of faith she had in her body not to let them get caught. And to let this man continue bestowing gift upon gift upon her every second his desire for her grew.

He touched her gently, deftly, as if he *knew* her. As if he knew exactly how far to go. When to apply pressure and when to pull away. A warm, melting weight made her body feel heavy. Pulling everything inwards towards his barely there contact.

Her breaths began to hitch in her throat. Her surroundings swarmed in on her. 'I can't,' she said, her voice a desperate plea.

'Yes, you bloody well can.' His voice became little more than a growl, and it only made her hotter still. 'You have no idea

Play the

Lucky Hearts Game

and get...

2 FREE BOOKS *and*
2 FREE MYSTERY GIFTS...
YOURS to KEEP!

yes! I have scratched off the silver card. Please send me my *2 FREE BOOKS* and *2 FREE mystery GIFTS* (gifts are worth about $10). I understand that I am under no obligation to purchase any books as explained on the back of this card.

Scratch Here!
then look below to see what your cards get you...
2 Free Books & 2 Free Mystery Gifts!

▼ DETACH AND MAIL CARD TODAY! ▼

© 2007 HARLEQUIN ENTERPRISES LIMITED
® and ™ are trademarks owned and used by the trademark owner and/or its licensee.

306 HDL ESRX   106 HDL ESVA

FIRST NAME   LAST NAME

ADDRESS

APT.#   CITY

STATE/PROV.   ZIP/POSTAL CODE   (H-P-09/08)

Twenty-one gets you
2 FREE BOOKS and
2 FREE MYSTERY GIFTS!

Twenty gets you
2 FREE BOOKS!

Nineteen gets you
1 FREE BOOK!

TRY AGAIN!

Offer limited to one per household and not valid to current subscribers of Harlequin Presents® books. All orders subject to approval.
Your Privacy – Harlequin Books is committed to protecting your privacy. Our Privacy Policy is available online at
www.eHarlequin.com or upon request from the Reader Service. From time to time we make our lists of customers available to
reputable third parties who may have a product or service of interest to you. If you would prefer us not to share your name
and address, please check here. ☐

The Reader Service — Here's how it works:

Accepting your 2 free books and 2 free mystery gifts places you under no obligation to buy anything. You may keep the books and gifts and return the shipping statement marked "cancel". If you do not cancel, about a month later we'll send you 6 additional books and bill you just $4.05 each in the U.S. or $4.74 each in Canada, plus 25¢ shipping & handling per book and applicable taxes if any.* That's the complete price and at a savings of at least 15% off the cover price, it's quite a bargain! You may cancel at any time, but if you choose to continue, every month we'll send you 6 more books which you may either purchase at the discount price or return to us and cancel your subscription.

*Terms and prices subject to change without notice. Sales tax applicable in N.Y. Canadian residents will be charged applicable provincial taxes and GST. Offer not valid in Quebec. Credit or debit balances in a customer's account(s) may be offset by any other outstanding balance owed by or to the customer. Please allow 4 to 6 weeks for delivery. Offer available while quantities last.

If offer card is missing write to: The Harlequin Reader Service, 3010 Walden Ave., P.O. Box 1867, Buffalo NY 14240-1867

BUSINESS REPLY MAIL
FIRST-CLASS MAIL   PERMIT NO. 717   BUFFALO, NY

POSTAGE WILL BE PAID BY ADDRESSEE

HARLEQUIN READER SERVICE
3010 WALDEN AVE
PO BOX 1867
BUFFALO NY 14240-9952

NO POSTAGE
NECESSARY
IF MAILED
IN THE
UNITED STATES

how much I want shove this table aside and lunge at you and sink my teeth into that spot where your neck meets your shoulder. I have truly never seen anything so gorgeous in my entire life. The only way to stop that kind of racket from happening is to give in and let me do this instead.'

With that he pushed her panties aside so that his whole hand could cup her, his every finger could move with her as she moved with him. As she tried so hard to keep still while instinct took over and she gave into it as he'd told her to do. She slid forward, let her head press against the back of the seat, and trusted him.

And in that moment she knew that even if she lost this round, she won.

It was enough for the last shreds of her self-control to fade away like a mirage in the far distance of her subconscious. She bit her lip to stop from making any sound as every warm, delicate sensation built to a tremendous crescendo before everything turned a blinding white and she dissolved into a million tiny little pieces.

It felt like hours later when his hand tidied her panties before sliding away. When her breathing returned to normal. When she could see more than a swirl of colours behind her eyelids.

'Are you ready to choose your orders, sir?' a male voice called from somewhere to Chelsea's left.

Her eyes flung open to find Damien leaning back in his chair, cool as you please. 'Are you ready, Chels?' he asked.

He smiled at her then, a smile that would have seemed to any onlooker as though he was politeness himself. But she saw the pulse in his neck throb and his fingers clench the menu.

She pressed her knees back together and brought herself fully upright. It took for her to lick her lips and blink about a dozen times to collect herself into a position where she could find a word to say, but she got there in the end.

'Steak,' she said, ignoring her menu. 'I was promised steak.'

'Twice over,' Damien said, closing the menu and passing it to the waiter. 'I'll have mine rare.'

'How would you like yours cooked, ma'am?'

'Well done for me. To the point of being dangerously dark. Tell the chef to take all the time he needs to cook it.'

The waiter glanced up at her, then at Damien, the slightest of frowns as he tried to decipher what he was missing in the conversation. But when they continued making eyes at one another across the table he figured it was better left unknown. 'Very good,' he said, then walked away.

Chelsea tugged her skirt back into place with one hand and reached for a glass of water with the other. She took a long sip, not quite knowing where to look. But when her eyes eventually found Damien's, what she saw there eased her mind.

His eyes were the colour of a starless midnight sky. His hair ruffled as though he'd just run frustrated fingers through it. He wanted her even more. And she had the distinct impression this wasn't even close to being as good as it was going to get.

She had to take a deep breath before throwing him a quick, 'So what's the party trick? I'm still waiting.'

And with that he burst into laughter. Loud, rolling waves that took the slow burn lingering in her limbs and blew them into the beginnings of a wildfire.

'I'm going to freshen up,' he said, sliding out from behind the table. But before he left he leaned down to kiss her. Holding her chin with enough force that as his mouth moved over hers she melted in his hold. Their tongues slid past one another. Their body heat intermingled.

He pulled away looking down into her eyes. 'Delight,' he said. 'An unmitigated delight.'

Then he was gone, easing past the Ficus and through the labyrinthine tables and out of sight.

* * *

By the time dessert was almost over Damien cleared his throat and Chelsea glanced up at him, playing with the last strawberry, pushing it around with her fork and drowning in his dark eyes and chiselled jaw line.

He wiped his mouth with his napkin, then said, 'Well, I for one think this has been a remarkable first date. What do you say to a second?'

His words hit somewhere deep inside her like a flaming arrow shot from point-blank range. It was enough for her to put her fork down, sit back in her chair, and fold her arms.

'I'm undecided,' she said. 'Though they do say it's the last five pages of a book that sell the next one.'

'Talk about putting pressure on a guy,' he joked, but for a moment he seemed genuinely surprised that she was keeping her options open. But he recovered remarkably quickly and said, 'Time to turn the spotlight, I think. I've told you far more about my screwball family than you could ever want to know, so now it's your turn. What's your family like, apart from felonious?'

She coughed out a laugh, her turn to be surprised by him. 'One sister. She was Kensington London to my Chelsea London until she very smartly married a guy called Greg Hurley. I blame my mother, who named us then left. My father died when I was sixteen.'

'I'm sorry.'

'Don't be. Neither of us have followed in either of their footsteps. Though Kensey did sell life insurance for a while. I'm sure there are many who would consider that a scam.'

'One I'm afraid shadows my own family name. My father owns Universal Life,' he said, naming one of the largest insurance companies in Australia.

Chelsea blanched. She'd known Damien was one of the bright and shiny ones, but he was a Halliburton of *those*

Halliburtons? He was beyond a New Uniform type. Half the buildings in his school were likely named after his ancestors while her father had been a scab on the face of existence and she had no clue if her mother was even still alive.

Enough was enough. She put her fingers to her mouth and whistled loud enough to grab the attention of a passing waiter, as well as the five tables in between. 'The bill, please,' she told him, 'and the faster it comes the more my friend here will tip.'

As Damien helped her from her seat he whispered in her ear, 'If you only knew how much that acid tongue of yours turns me on I'm afraid you'd only bite it.'

He was dead right; she didn't say another word, even as she quickly slid a small package from the pocket of her coat and left it with the hostess to give to Carrie.

Once they sorted out whose phone was whose, Damien held open the glass door for her and led her outside. It was dark. Cold. Her breath expelled in short white puffs of air. She stomped her feet against the cold pavement and waited for him to join her.

He walked to her side, rubbing his hands together. 'So,' he said.

'So,' she said back through cold lips. 'This has been some day.'

'One I don't think I'll easily forget.'

She glanced sideways; her gaze caught with his and held. So blue. Her heart did some kind of acrobatics in her chest and, though she knew it was a bad idea, she desperately wanted him to ask her out again. *Again.*

'I bet you didn't picture being here twice in a day when you woke up this morning,' she said, giving him time.

He laughed. 'Ah, no. I think I may have pictured meetings, phone calls, working through lunch, leaving the office way past dark, taking more work home and falling into bed some time after midnight.'

Bed... At the word *bed* his voice dropped, and her nerves danced beneath her skin.

'How about you?' he asked.

'Believe it or not you took the words right out of my mouth.'

Mouth... At the word *mouth* his gaze dropped to hers. It felt dry, in need of a quick lap of her tongue. As though he knew the self-control she was struggling against Damien smiled, abundantly confident in his sexual power.

But it didn't make Chelsea feel like smiling. Her lungs felt tight, her nerve endings on fire, and her heart was beating so fast she thought it might pop fair through her chest.

Was he punishing her? Leaving it up to her to ask him back to her place for coffee and finish what they'd started because she'd been so blasé about the idea earlier? It *was* what her body was aching for her to do. It was practically screaming.

She was beginning to shake with the cold. She should just listen to her head, and kiss him on the cheek, and say goodnight. Or better yet goodbye.

But then she thought about what it would be like to go home to her empty apartment, where she would shiver for a good ten minutes until the central heating kicked in. And even when she was dressed in her comfy flannelette pyjamas and bed socks, she would still be alone.

So without a second thought she followed her instincts and reached out and grabbed two handfuls of glorious soft wool coat, stood on tiptoes, and kissed him full on the mouth. Giving everything she had.

As though he'd merely been waiting for her to make a move, he immediately wrapped his hand behind her neck, pulling her closer still. Her eyes closed, she breathed out through her nose and once again let down her guard and let him in.

He opened his coat and scooped her inside. She slid her arms around his waist and sank against him. And in his hold she felt warm, secure, desired, beautiful, and brimming with power. And maybe, just maybe, this thing that had sprung up so suddenly between them had the potential to be far more than what it seemed.

A wolf-whistle from some young punk in a passing car pulled Chelsea out of her reverie. She slowly ended the kiss and pulled back just far enough to draw breath. Hard breaths, heavy breaths, but not nearly as hard and heavy as those belonging to the man in her arms.

'Come home with me,' she said, her voice husky and soft.

He swallowed and leaned his forehead against hers. For so many seconds they felt like minutes. Until she began to wonder if he'd heard her at all. She prepared herself to ask again when he finally said:

'Not tonight, Chelsea.'

Her blood turned to cold sludge in her veins. Now she just wanted to get out of there and fast. She began by uncurling her fingers from his coat.

'You have no idea how much I want to,' Damien said, not letting her go just yet, pulling her closer until she felt the physical evidence of his words. 'But I have an early meeting. And after spending every spare minute on the phone to you, I have a pile of papers to catch up on at home before then.'

He reached out and tucked a lock of hair behind her ear. 'Any chance I can get your phone number, though?'

Chelsea thought about telling him where he could stick her number. But now more than anything she wanted to walk away feeling sophisticated, or at least hoping he saw her as such. Not used and shattered and weak and self-destructive for trusting him so quickly when he'd given her no real cause to apart from seeming too good to be true.

She reached into her purse, pulled out a pen, grabbed his hand, turned it over and wrote her mobile number on his warm palm and then began backing away.

'So that's goodnight?' he asked, arms outstretched, broad form haloed by the light spilling from inside the restaurant.

She kept backing away, her heels clacking on the concrete beneath her feet, putting more and more distance between them. 'You'd better get home quickly if you don't want my number to rub away.'

His arms dropped to his sides and, the further she went, the darker and more shadowed his face became until she could no longer see the expression in his eyes. And just like that he was no more to her than a beautiful stranger again. She would do well to remember it.

He pushed his coat aside, reached into his jacket pocket and pulled out his phone. Lifting his hand towards the streetlight, he punched in a bunch of numbers.

Her phone vibrated in her pocket and out rang the theme tune from *The Mary Tyler Moore Show*—a show she and Kensey had loved watching the few months growing up they'd had access to a television. Despite the fact that she was doing her best to disentangle herself from him, she answered it.

'Hello?'

'Chelsea, hi. It's Damien.'

'Damien who?' She felt his smile from twenty good metres away. She *didn't* know him, but it sure felt as if she did. Knew him, liked him, and much more... She picked up her pace.

'Ah, the age-old question. Right up there with who am I? Why am I here? What's my favourite colour? Now you have my number in your phone you can call me back some time in order to find out.'

She watched him flip his phone shut, a flat tone buzzed in her ear. She flipped hers shut as well and slid it back into her purse. From halfway down the block he was now half hidden by the light pedestrian traffic.

She saw him raise a hand goodbye, but she just turned and walked away, knowing there was no way on God's green earth she'd be calling him.

His second rebuff in one night well and truly restored the temporary kink in her self-control.

CHAPTER EIGHT

'Sir?'

Damien's vision cleared to find Mindy looking at him expectantly. 'I'm sorry, what?'

'Are you ready for our reports?' she asked.

He glanced at the clock on the wall. It was just after seven a.m. He looked around the oval conference table at his team, who all had mugs of steaming hot coffee in their hands to combat the early hour, and looks of faint concern in their eyes that their intrepid leader obviously wasn't firing on all cylinders.

'Your reports,' he said. 'Of course. Go. Shoot.'

'Right,' Mindy said, then launched into a bullet-point breakdown of every news report of the night before that she thought might be relevant to the upcoming day's trades.

Damien's leg started shaking at the lead story. He'd torn off the ends of his fingernails on one hand by the time they hit the special interest section. He almost made it all the way through the weather, before he scraped his chair back so loud the whole room went quiet.

Caleb mouthed, *What are you doing?*

'I'll be back in a sec. Keep going.'

And then he tore from the room.

'I have an early meeting,' he said aloud, repeating the words that had been thumping in his head the whole night through as he'd lain awake on Caleb's couch, alone, wishing he could turn back the clock and follow Chelsea wherever she led.

He *had* had an early meeting as he did every day of the week and it had never stopped him from indulging in night-time action before.

But when Chelsea had asked him to come home with her, something about her, about the ingenuous intensity of her preceding goodnight kiss, had spooked him enough for him to tell a beautiful and willing woman who'd had him wound up as tight as a new spring, 'Not tonight.'

He'd been, of all things, honourable. And then somewhere in the middle of the night, as he'd tossed and turned on Caleb's couch, he'd decided honour could go jump.

So what if she smelt like sunshine not perfume? So what if she was soft, and vulnerable, and honest and nothing about her screamed one-night stand?

He had to see her again.

He found himself in the lift and pressed the button for the ground floor. He slid his phone from his pocket and keyed in her phone number, which was now already imprinted on his brain like a brand. It rang. And rang. And rang.

The lift binged, he was in the foyer and moving through the revolving glass doors to Collins Street. The autumn chill seeped beneath his shirt, tie and suit trousers in a Melbourne minute.

Damien gripped the phone in preparation of slamming it closed, when the ringing tone stopped and a familiar voice said, 'Good morning, Damien.'

'Chelsea.' He turned down a side alley and out of the way of passers-by and the bluster shooting down the Collins Street wind tunnel. 'Hi. Hi. Good morning yourself.'

He slapped a hand across his eyes. *Okay, so now that you have her what are you going to do with her?*

'You'll have to be quick,' she said, her voice far cooler than his. 'I'm literally on my way out the door. Early meeting.'

Well, he deserved that. 'Of course. No worries. I just… I wanted to call to say hello.'

Smooth. You are truly some kind of Valentino. She'll be quivering at the knees right this second.

'Would have been cheaper to send a text message. Or a postcard. How about next time you get the urge you post me a letter? People don't write nearly enough nowadays.'

'Chelsea—'

'I get it,' she said. 'Truly. You don't have to ease your conscience with some heartfelt rendition of "it's not you it's me". Yesterday was one out of the box. And last night was something else entirely. But all in all it was a story with which to delight your friends come Friday night happy hour. You're not the first, and I'm sure despite my best efforts you won't be the last, man I meet who'll have an early meeting.'

Again he was hit with a wave of absolute vulnerability. Most of the time she came across as so gung-ho. So unruffled. But he could hear, as clear as if she'd said the words out loud, that he'd done it again. He'd hurt her.

But awful as that was, as much as it was exactly what he'd been trying to avoid, the strength of her reaction gave him hope he might convince her to see him again. Once they were within touching distance he'd be in his element again and he'd know just how to make them both feel better.

He stopped pacing and planted his feet on the ground and stared hard at the graffiti-riddled brick wall of the alley. 'I haven't called to tell you I don't want to see you again, Chelsea.'

She remained silent. Her disbelief palpable.

He ran a hand through his hair. 'I don't know what kind of guys you've dated in the past, but for me this whole phone thing we have going on leaves a lot to be desired. Especially now that I find myself missing the Mary Tyler Moore ring tone.'

She laughed through her nose, or at least that was what it sounded like. He clung onto the small noise for dear life.

'Let me prove it to you. Let me take you out again tonight. I'll pick you up, I'll take you somewhere nice where there will be no waiters with nose rings or exposed bra straps, I'll pay and I'll escort you home like a regular old-fashioned date. No funny business.'

He crossed his fingers through the last part. He wanted funny business with her so much he could barely walk straight.

After a long pause she said, 'I don't mind nose rings. What I don't like is bad service. And small portions at exorbitant prices. And snooty uppity sorts who think themselves above other people.'

He had a feeling she was somehow referring to him, which didn't bode well for funny business so he chose to ignore it. 'Fine,' he said. 'I'll do my best to find somewhere suitable. Tattoos all round and at the first sign of snootiness we walk. And afterwards, well, we'll cross that bridge when we come to it. Okay?'

'Fine,' she said. She sounded as though she'd agreed against her will, but he had the feeling this woman didn't do anything against her will. Her will was even stronger than his. And her will said he'd done enough to have her want to see him again.

He punched the air and let out a silent whoop.

'Excellent. Let's say seven o'clock. Text me your address as I'm nowhere near a piece of paper—'

'You do know your phone has a notebook function?'

'That's nice. But I actually know how to retrieve a text message.' He thought he did anyway. He'd better get back to the office just in case.

He looked around and realised he was halfway down a hill heading goodness knew where. He headed up the hill hoping he'd remember which way to turn when he reached civilisation again. 'Does this thing have a Global Positioning System?'

'Of course it does.' She laughed again and this time it was softer, gentler, more forgiving. 'Someone ought to buy you a pocket-sized paper notebook for Christmas.'

'I'll add it to Santa's list,' he said. 'So, I'll see you at seven?'

'You will. Although I could just as easily send you to some deserted block as punishment for how you ended things last night.'

Damien grinned as he hit Collins Street and got his bearings and marched back towards the office. 'No,' he said. 'You like me far too much to do that.'

She didn't deny it. All she said was, 'Then don't be late.'

'I'll be so early I'll be embarrassing.'

'Bye, Damien.'

'See you soon, Chelsea.' Damien hung up only once he was sure the line was dead.

He pushed through the glass doors and jogged across the foyer, a newfound spring in his step. He knew that day he'd work as hard as ten men, to make up for the day before, and so that time would fly until he would be at her door.

And this time nothing, not cold feet, or honour, or guilt would stop him from happily taking from her whatever delights she readily offered.

Chelsea slowly hung up the phone. The only early meeting she had was with a cup of coffee and the newspaper.

She left the remains of both on the table in the kitchen nook at home, finished off the last bite of reheated leftover chicken teriyaki from a couple of nights before, then padded into her bedroom, disrobing as she headed towards the shower, wondering when exactly she'd become a masochist.

She'd gambled big three times in her life. Finishing high school via correspondence while she worked full-time in a pet-grooming business after her father died to help Kensey pay the rent. Taking over the business when her mentor retired. And buying out Kensey for this apartment.

All had given her the beginnings of stomach ulcers at first. But now…

She looked around her at the beautiful bedroom. Sunshine spilled through the small balcony window, a light breeze kissing the gauzy curtains. The opulent furnishings made the large space feel cosy. Her instincts had been dead on.

So what were her instincts telling her about Damien? That he was a creature of comfort who was emotionally unavailable. Not looking to fill any kind of void in his life with one woman.

She padded into the *en suite* and turned on the hot water, waiting until the room filled with heavenly steam before she cooled it down and slid under the invigorating spray.

But he was also a man who made her laugh. A man who made her able to forget her inhibitions and give herself to another person more intimately than she ever had.

Damien Halliburton was a man who just might be worth the gamble, or might yet prove her to be the greatest fool who ever walked the earth.

Right now she felt as if the odds were about even.

Just before seven o'clock that night, Damien walked up Flinders Lane pressing past clumps of scantily clad waifs spilling from funky restaurant doorways. He smiled at those who smiled at him first, but his steps did not falter. He was a man on a mission.

He looked up. Solid black wrought-iron balconies scattered the dark brick façade above. Several had light from inside spilling through translucent curtains, others yet trailed in blood-red bougainvillea. The building was unique and utterly charming. Much like the inhabitant he was here to see.

He straightened his tie, ran a hand over his hair, and paused with his finger over the doorbell of Chelsea's apartment, wondering what on earth this night might bring him. It wasn't as though any of this had gone according to plan so far.

He steeled himself, puffed out his chest, clutched at the bunch of lustrous orange tulips he'd bought for her and poked the button with as much force as his finger could take without breaking a bone.

After a few long seconds, the breathy sound of the intercom broke through the white noise of a city at play, and a husky voice answered, 'Hello?'

He checked he had the right apartment number, then leaned into the speaker. 'Chelsea, it's Damien.'

Another pause. 'Damien? Oh, heck, I'd completely forgotten.' And smoked three packets of cigarettes in a minute flat by the sound of her.

Then the gist of what she'd said sank in. Forgotten? When he'd rushed out of work the minute the markets had closed to make sure he wasn't a second late, she—

'Damien?'

'I'm still here,' he said, not bothering to hide his annoyance. 'Are you going to buzz me in?'

'I can't. I—'

'Don't tell me you're not ready,' he said, feeling more and

more frustrated at having to talk to her through a wall. They might as well have been on the phone. Again.

He didn't want that any more. He wanted to see her. Touch her. Smell her. Kiss her. Slide her clothes from her limbs. And to sink into her, to ease the ache that had built inside him since the first moment he'd looked into those golden brown eyes.

'I'm happy to wait for you to tidy up or pick an outfit or dab on perfume or whatever it is you have yet to do. Just let me in.'

'I…can't. Damien.' She paused. He even heard the sound shut off at the other end for a second before it came back on. 'The truth is I'm sick.'

'Sick,' he repeated, wondering if that was some kind of code, like washing her hair, or paying him back for the early-morning excuse after all.

Frustrated to the point of a painfully clenched jaw, he looked over his shoulder. Melbourne was alive all around him. Music pouring from restaurant speakers. Tables full of young women laughing and young men paying close attention. All he wanted was to be a part of that scene again.

Maybe this thing between them had been all too hard from day dot for a reason. The fates were telling him to leave her well enough alone. To reinvigorate his weary libido in another pair of willing arms.

'Damien?' her reedy voice said again, and he knew, despite what his instincts were blaring at him, something else inside him simply wouldn't let him leave.

'Chelsea,' he said, dropping his voice to its most persuasive level. 'Let. Me. In.'

The smoked-glass door beside him clicked and he grabbed it and yanked it open. He shot through the marble lobby, giving brief nods to the octogenarian couple leaving the lift as he entered it. The art deco lifts took far too long to take him to the third floor. But when he got there her front door was ajar.

He took another deep breath and pushed it open to find Chelsea pacing the floor of a one-bedroom apartment over-stuffed with furniture and books and knick-knacks and floral patterns so rich he practically had to squint to block them out.

She whooshed past him, a blur of tartan flannelette and bare feet. The frivolous hot-pink glitter on her toenails had him rooted to the floor. It took her husky voice to cut through his little daydream.

'I didn't want you to see me like this.'

He dragged his gaze upwards from her sexy toes past her baggy clothes to find her hair sprouted from a messy pony-tail atop her head. She wore not a lick of make-up. Her eyes were huge pools of muted gold, her lips overly pink against her pale skin. She looked warm and ruffled and ready for bed. All over his body his skin tightened until it felt a size too small.

'I'm never sick,' she wailed. 'I'm so careful about everything as I can't afford to be sick. I take multi-vitamins. I drink two litres of water a day. I wash my hands so much I'm in danger of being compulsive. Though when you deal with the kind of stuff I deal with on a daily basis hand-washing is a must. I—' She came to an abrupt halt and began to breathe deep through her nose, her nostrils flaring, her cheeks bright pink.

She looked so wild. He wanted nothing more than to stride over to her and drag her into his arms and kiss her. His hands gripped so hard on the flowers he felt the stems crush.

But then her skin lost all semblance of colour. Her lips turned grey and she bolted. And the wretched sounds coming from her direction left him in no doubt that she was sincerely as sick as she'd said she was.

Still standing in the entrance, he had not one clue as to what to do. Surely he should go. She'd tried to warn him. And it wasn't as though he had any kind of qualifications. Did throwing up call for chicken soup? Or was that lemon and ginger tea?

When after a good three minutes he'd heard nothing of her at all, an overwhelming wave of concern that she'd gone and done something foolish like pass out overrode any kind of squeamishness he might have had. It seemed his gallantry was not yet at an end.

He closed the door behind him with a soft click, placed the flowers on the hall stand, shucked off his jacket, leaving it hanging over the back of an overstuffed couch upholstered in some awful pink-rose fabric, and rolled up his sleeves.

She wouldn't be the first girl whose hair he'd held off her face in a time of need. But she was the first girl he'd ever eaten humble pie for, and he had come all this way to see her so if this was how their second date was meant to play out, so be it.

Chelsea awoke with the thin morning sun teasing pink and pretty through the gauzy curtains of her bedroom window.

Her head felt like a bag of sand—dry, coarse and far too heavy to lift. Her mouth tasted as if she hadn't cleaned her teeth in a week. She put a shaky hand over her eyes and sat up.

When she opened them she saw a folded newspaper on her bedside table. A plate of dry crackers and crumbs proving some of them had been eaten during the night. A single perfect orange tulip in a water-filled spaghetti jar. And just like that her night came swimming back to her.

Damien.

While she'd spent most of the night sleeping on the couch or with her head over the toilet bowl, he'd been there. Not hovering, not mothering, just there. Watching TV. Reading a magazine by the window with the blinds open and the city view painting its golden light upon his gorgeous profile. And had he really made her toast with Vegemite, cooked himself dinner from the pathetic contents of her fridge *and* loaded her dishwasher?

She pulled herself from her bed, and realised she had no idea how she'd ended up there and in a frilly sleeveless neck-to-knee white cotton nightie she hadn't worn in years.

She grabbed her plush cream robe from the knob on the side of her cheval mirror, wrapped herself in it, tight, then headed out into the lounge room.

But all was quiet. Her kitchen was clean. And she was most definitely alone.

She poured a large glass of tap water, then headed to the lounge-room balcony. She opened the glass door a smidge, just enough to let in some morning sunshine, air, and comforting noise to drown out the plethora of embarrassing images in her head.

Whatever would she say to the guy when she saw him again? If she ever saw him again.

She dropped her head into her hands with a groan.

Damien stood below Chelsea's apartment building holding a bag filled with croissants, cheese and bacon rolls and three different types of fresh bread as well as two steaming hot black coffees, with his mobile pressed to his ear.

'Yeah, hello,' Caleb said at the other end of the line.

'It's Damien. I need you to do me a favour.'

After a loud long yawn Caleb said, 'Name it, buddy.'

'I need you to take the morning meeting today.'

Silence.

'Caleb?'

'Yeah, I'm still here. Just needed a moment to check the

number on my screen, make sure it was really you. You're going to be late?'

'Yes, I'm going to be late.'

'You realise it's a weekday, right?'

'Caleb—'

'Wow. I feel like I should commemorate this day with some kind of plaque, or parade, or something.'

'Commemorate by holding the morning meeting.'

'So what time will you be in?'

Damien glanced up at the third-storey balcony, which he now knew looked out from Chelsea's small lounge-room. Fine white curtains fluttered in a light breeze, meaning she was up, padding about her apartment in just about the sexiest night attire he had ever come across.

'Not sure,' he said. 'Later. Maybe. I'll call you.'

'But, Damien—'

Damien tore his gaze away, used the key he'd pilfered from Chelsea's hall table, and walked into the foyer. 'Let the gang talk. Any info that sounds interesting, use. Check on each trader during the day, touch base with each of the platinum clients in my Rolodex, leave your office door open, and try to refrain from fondling any of the staff. I trust you.'

'I'm not sure you should.'

Damien jabbed the lift button with his elbow.

'Are you in the hospital?' Caleb asked. 'Have you been kidnapped? Does someone have a gun to your head?'

Damien watched his reflection on the inside of the silver-panelled lift doors. 'I'm fine. In one piece. I just have something more important I need to do right now.'

'Like what?'

'I'm with Chelsea.'

Caleb paused. 'The hot get-back-on-the-horse cat lady?'

Damien breathed out slowly through his nose. 'If you call her that again I'll slap you silly.'

'Why?'

Why. *Why?* Damien ran a hand over his eyes and counted to ten. 'Because it's rude, that's why.'

'You're playing hookey for her? You met her, what, five minutes ago? And now she's what? Your girlfriend? Did you give her your varsity jacket?'

'Caleb. She's not my girlfriend. She's a girl in need of a helping hand. Nothing more.'

'Right. Though take one piece of advice from a veteran in the ways of the heart, won't you?'

'And that is…?'

'Be careful.'

His own words from the night before came swimming back to him. 'Careful about what, exactly?'

'This girl. You know who you are. Who your parents are. What they expect of you. You know what you have to offer. Just be careful about how and why she's managed to get her claws into you so quick. Be sure about your reasons, and hers.'

'Caleb,' he warned.

'I'm your best mate. Everything I say I say out of love. I've known you for umpteen years. Our parents play gin-soaked tennis together on a weekly basis, and that's a lifestyle I intend to protect so that when I grow in need of my first facelift I can take on the mantle of that fantastic life where they leave off. And I want you there by my side. Well, three or four blondes to my left, but in sight all the same.'

The lift binged. Damien's reflection wavered and split. The cream panelled walls of the hallway leading to Chelsea's apartment appeared before him. Images of sleep-ruffled caramel-blonde hair, wide golden eyes, and slim pale arms lifting trustingly so that he could slide a nightie over her half naked form swarmed over him and he pushed Caleb's words far to the back of his head.

'Gotta go,' he said, then hung up.

Chelsea heard a noise. She spun towards the front door to see the handle moving. She could hear keys jangling. Her heart thundered in her chest as she simply stood there staring at the door waiting for the intruder to enter.

It was Damien. Tall, dark, slick, and tidy in a dark grey pin-striped suit with a white shirt and deep blue, soft patterned tie the exact same colour as his eyes. A bakery bag was clenched between his teeth, and he held a cardboard tray of coffee she could smell from all the way across the room. She tidied her hair as she said, 'You scared the life out of me. How on earth did you get in here?'

Damien threw her keys back onto the hall table and pulled the bag from between his teeth. 'I stole your keys. I thought you might be up for some breakfast.'

She wrapped her arms around her stomach, less from any kind of modesty and more to quell the tumbling sensation rock-eting through her at the very sight of him. At the knowledge that he *had* been there the night before. Had come expecting a date he'd had no doubt would this time end up horizontal, had instead found her a sick mess, fed her, undressed her, and stayed.

'Hungry?' he asked.

Her empty stomach rumbled. She took one small step his way. 'What have you got?'

'Just about one of everything from the bakery downstairs.' He dumped the paper bag and coffee tray on the table in the kitchen nook, then headed into her kitchen where he found her dinner plates, first try.

She plopped into a chair and tucked her knees against her chest, wrapping her arms tight around her calves as she watched him pull out cutlery and napkins.

She'd never had a man in her kitchen before. Well, apart from Kensey's Greg, who usually stood there looking lost until one or the other of them sent him scooting into the lounge while they looked after his every need.

But Damien looked so at home. He looked...right. *So* right something shifted behind her ribs with all the force and might and destructive power of a newly unstable tectonic plate until deeply affectionate warmth bled through her body like lava.

'So what happened to you last night?' Damien asked as he joined her at the table.

She pretended to pick at a small stain on the Chantilly lace tablecloth. 'I'm not sure. It could have been a bug from a dog I washed up after a couple of days ago. Or maybe it was the leftover chicken teriyaki I had for breakfast yesterday.'

She glanced up and caught him watching her from over the top of his cup of coffee. All beautiful eyes, and expensive clothes and perfect hair. And attraction. Unguarded attraction so palpable it lay upon her shoulders like a warm blanket. She broke eye contact lest he saw a heightened version of the same emotion stampeding through her.

'I...I don't know how to thank you for last night,' she said. 'For the toast. And the tidying. And the company. That was most certainly above and beyond second-date duties.'

He smiled, and the disturbing shift inside her only deepened, making her feel as if her chest were now nothing more than a gaping hole waiting for him to fill it up. 'My pleasure,' he said. 'Now eat up.'

She reached forward and grabbed a croissant, eating a layer at a time. 'No early-morning meeting today then?'

He grabbed a roll and lathered it with butter. Then glanced up, stunning her silly with the cocky smile in his brilliant blue eyes. 'There is,' he said with a smile. 'Only this time I'm not going to be there.'

'Oh. And that's okay? You can do that?'

'As it turns out when you're the boss, you can do whatever you damn well please. And you? Are you going to do the sensible thing and call in sick?'

She hadn't even thought that far. She still felt weak after her night-long purge, but she'd worked through worse. 'I have no idea what kind of day I have today. But Phyllis would have bluetoothed me the appointment list before I left work last night.'

Damien looked at her as if she were speaking Swahili.

'My phone,' she explained. 'Have you seen it?'

'On the coffee-table, I do believe,' he said.

They both stood at the same time and made a move in that direction. Then stopped, staring at one another. He was close enough she could smell the scent of fresh bread on his clothes. She could see the soft haze of dark stubble on his cheeks.

His gaze flickered over her hair, her cheeks, her lips, which felt moist with croissant grease. And he leaned towards her. To kiss her. She could see it in his eyes, the set of his jaw, the tension in his shoulders.

She leaned back and pressed a hand to his chest and said out of the corner of her mouth, 'I have the worst morning breath I have ever known.'

His eyes narrowed, as though he was thinking through whether he gave a damn, before he leaned away from her. Her hand dropped. And as soon as it did he was there, gathering her close, pressing his lips against hers.

She closed her eyes and let him, her limbs relaxing with every second he encouraged her to open her mouth to his.

When he pulled back he was smiling down at her with such desire she could have whimpered. 'I've wanted to do that since I first saw you last night.'

'Worth the wait?' she asked.

'You tell me.'

Instead she bit her lips, hiding her fuzzy teeth and just as fuzzy breath as she extricated herself from his divine embrace.

He made his way back to the kitchen table and she stumbled into the lounge, where she grabbed her phone and her thumbs ran purposefully over the keys until she found her appointments list. The day was as full as it ever was.

But with Damien lounging on the other side of her kitchen table, his gaze still lingering on her lips, not looking as if he had any intention of going anywhere this time, she pressed a number on her speed dial and waited for Phyllis to answer.

'You're not in until ten,' Phyllis chastised.

'Actually I'm calling to let you know I won't be in at all.' As she said the words out loud her legs began to shake, as though they could finally give into how weak she truly felt. She sat on the couch.

'You okay?'

'Sick as a dog, actually. But a day ought to do me.'

'Right. Good. Don't worry about a thing. I'll handle everything. Just you wait and see. I can manage this place, no worries. Or a place just like it if there's one on offer. So, you signed the papers for the loan yet?'

'Ah, no. Not yet.

'But you will.'

'I yet may.'

'Hmm. Well, rest up. Take care. Lie down. Eat well. Don't do anything to wear yourself out, okay?'

She glanced at Damien, who had his right leg crossed over

his left as he read the morning paper. His pinstriped trousers strained against the muscle of his thighs. His pale shirt stretched across his broad torso. His tongue darted out to catch a crumb on the edge of his lip. And all Chelsea wanted to do was crawl up onto his lap and wear herself out thoroughly.

'I'll see you tomorrow,' she said, then rang off.

Damien closed the paper before glancing up at her, pinning her to the lounge-chair with his dark gaze. 'Day off?'

She nodded, and turned her phone over and over in her palm.

He glanced at the coffee and bakery feast on the table, then back at her. 'This is a first for me.'

'Me too,' she admitted.

He picked up a piece of hot flaky bread and took a bite. And only after he'd swallowed it down did he break the silence again. Saying, 'Whatever will we do to fill in the time?'

CHAPTER NINE

CHELSEA again woke with light filtering through the backs of her eyelids. Only this time she was curled up on the pink floral couch in the front room wearing velour track pants and a long sleeved T-shirt. She blinked to clear her fuzzy vision and the display on the mobile phone on the coffee-table read 4:15. She could only assume it was in the afternoon.

The TV was on with the sound turned down low, which wasn't all that unusual. She liked having the TV on when home so that she didn't feel as if she was alone.

What was unusual was that her head was resting on a pair of strong male thighs.

She peeked up into Damien's face. He was completely immersed in the action on the TV. She glanced back, and over the half-empty bowl of popcorn realised he was watching Doris Day sling it out with Howard Keel in *Calamity Jane*. She bit back the laughter that bubbled into her throat.

She moved slightly then, trying to extricate herself before he realised she was awake. But when she went to move the arm beneath her head she realised she was trapped. Her hand was tucked neatly between his warm thighs. She sent a quick prayer to the heavens in the hopes that was as far as it had ventured while she slept.

She managed to slide her hand less than an inch before his thighs clamped down. Her gaze shot northward to meet with a pair of smiling blue eyes.

'Good afternoon,' Damien said, his deep sexy voice washing over her like a shower of warm milk.

'Hi,' she said, her voice soft and croaky with sleep.

'Sweet dreams?'

The last hazy remains of what had been a pretty hot and detailed dream still lingered on the edge of her mind. She looked away before he realised he had been the star. 'How long was I out?'

'A couple of hours.'

'Wow. I haven't had a nap during the day since… I can't remember when.'

'You needed it.'

She tried to sit up again, and his thighs only clamped down tighter. 'May I have my hand back?'

'Don't know how I feel about that.'

'Well, I have *no* feeling left from my wrist down, so it won't do you any good to keep it there.'

Damien held eye contact for a few heated seconds longer before slowly releasing his grip. She slid her hand from the space and brought it out into the cold of the open air.

She sat up, rubbing at her fingers, but there was no way she could regather the kind of warmth they'd felt being so near his skin.

He grabbed the remote from the coffee-table to turn off the TV.

'Oh, no,' she said, 'don't stop on my account. You a big Doris Day fan?'

Damien's eyes narrowed, piercing her until her lethargic heartbeat kicked up to a jogging rate. 'I had been watching

Ocean's Eleven, the Rat Pack version. This simply came on afterwards and I knew if I moved to get the remote I'd wake you.'

'How benevolent.'

'Just call me Nurse Halliburton. I seem to have a flare for it. Odd considering the only time anyone in my family has been in need of a hospital has been the rehab kind.' A smile pulled at his cheeks.

She tucked her feet up onto the couch and wrapped her arms around her knees for protection. But nothing could have protected her from the rush of feelings when he reached out and ran a finger down her cheek.

'My trousers have left a crease mark,' he said.

Her hand flew to her face. She could only imagine how she must have looked. Even after her long hot bath, and the three times she'd cleaned her teeth, her hair must by now have again looked a mess. Her eyes puffy. Pink-cheeked with the image of wool trousers branded into her face like some kind of overfamiliar tattoo. She let her hair fall forward to act as a curtain.

Damien's hand reached out again, pushing her hair behind her ear.

'Chelsea,' he said, his voice insistent. He looked so deep into her eyes she could scarcely breathe. His hand continued sweeping her hair over her ear, and along her neck. Over and over again. 'There's something I want to say to you, to make clear, before you fall asleep on me again.'

Her hand dropped to her lap. 'Okay.'

'I wanted to tell you, now, while we're here alone, with no distractions, bar Doris Day's finest hour on film, that sitting here, watching you sleep like an angel in my lap, I have come to the conclusion…'

He stopped and took a deep breath. Chelsea held hers until her lungs felt as if they were about to burst.

'I can't go another day without making love to you, Miss London.'

Chelsea's heart thundered in her chest as hard as she'd ever remembered feeling it thunder. The reciprocal words caught in her throat as pride and fear and hope and history egged her to hold her cards close to her chest. She'd never felt like this before in her whole life. Never experienced this kind of euphoria just by looking into another person's eyes. Each moment with him was a gamble with the chances of losing her guarded heart to him becoming greater with every passing moment. Nevertheless she gave into temptation and threw the dice.

'I want nothing more either, Mr Halliburton.'

He cupped her cheek, held her gaze and said, 'Then I also need you to know that I recently came out of my last relationship just shy of bloodshed. I don't plan to bore you with the gory details, but suffice it to say I'm not on the hunt for someone new to fill that place in my life.'

Chelsea swallowed hard, but Damien kept eye contact so she couldn't move.

'But,' he continued, 'I can't get you out of my mind. Your face, your lips, your skin haunts me and I can't deny that I want you.'

Chelsea's instincts screamed at her to listen and listen hard. He was openly admitting he wasn't in the market for permanence or responsibility. It wasn't just all in her head. Now was her chance to pull out, before she became the next in line to bleed for him.

But as she looked into his beautiful eyes she knew it was already too late. The temptation of him was simply too great. She reached out and ran a trembling finger over his lips. Every second seemed to stretch out before her, longer and longer until he leaned slowly in, and placed his lips upon hers.

It was the sweetest kiss of her life. His mouth gently moved against hers, coaxing more and more from her with every touch. And every conscious thought, every warring emotion, slipped away bar the feel of the man at her side.

He tasted of fresh roasted coffee and hazelnuts. Any hint of cologne from the night before had been replaced by the smell of pure warm male skin. The slight stubble on his chin rasped lightly against her chin, so that the goose-bumps trailing every inch of exposed skin did not for one second let up.

As the emotions inside her swelled to breaking-point, she pulled away the tiniest possible amount, and whispered, 'What if I'm contagious?'

His breath whispered against her lips. 'I'm willing to take the chance if you are.'

She looked into his eyes, and knew he was asking more of her than the possibility of sharing germs. He was asking her to take a chance on him, to let this kiss play out to its inevitable conclusion. He was asking her to dream big, damn the consequences.

She took a long slow breath, and nodded.

He blinked, just once and the deal was sealed.

This time when his lips met hers it was with more pressure, more urgency, and she couldn't have pulled away if she'd tried. Not that she wanted to try. All she wanted was to sink into him. To lose herself and find herself all at once.

Her hand moved beneath the hair at the back of his neck, sliding into the soft thick texture the way she'd wanted to ever since she'd first laid eyes on him. And she moved until she was lying on his lap, his strong grip holding her upright.

Then she opened her mouth to him and with it her powerless heart.

The kiss went on for ever, as they got to know one another's taste, and feel, and the particular things that made each other shiver and sigh.

Finally, his hand moved down her back, sliding along her spine until she curved into him. He reached the top of her track pants and didn't stop there. His hand dived beneath the waistline and managed to find skin on its first try.

His large warm palm cupped her left cheek and lifted her gently towards him. Deeper into his arms. If he was looking for a new way to make her shiver and sigh he'd found it.

She let her own hands drop to blindly find the buttons of his shirt. The kiss didn't let up as she undid each one and pushed the starched cotton off his shoulders, her hands stroking over hot, rolling muscles of his arms, which were far more beautiful than she'd even imagined.

As her hands moved around to the front, to course over his perfect chest, scraping against a smattering of dark, curling hair until her fingernails reached the fly of his trousers, Damien's hands slid up to grip hers, pulling everything to a halt.

The kiss broke apart so suddenly the two of them came up gulping for air.

'What's wrong?' she asked, turning her fingernails into her palms. If he rejected her for a third time she'd never forgive herself for being so consciously imprudent. For trusting a man who'd all but told her she shouldn't.

He shook his head, his eyes so dark she couldn't have guessed they were blue if she didn't know better.

'No?' she asked, wondering what she could possibly have done wrong.

'Yes,' he said. 'God yes. Just. Well. Hell.' With that he scooped her up in his arms.

She let out a whoop as her legs were flung into the air and her arms instinctively wrapped tight about his neck. And when he began to jog, no, run, into the bedroom she laughed so hard she was sure Mrs Luchek next door would have heard her had she not been away.

Chelsea took about half a second to worry if the bed was made before she landed upon it with a bounce. 'Whoa. I think I felt the earth move.'

Damien said nothing. He just stood at the end of the bed with his white business shirt open and hanging off his shoulders like a pirate on the front of an old romance novel. His breaths rose and fell in great slow moves and her mouth went completely dry. He was, quite simply, the sexiest man to ever walk the face of the earth.

He slid the shirt from his back and let it drop where it fell. If his body had felt beautiful it looked, if at all possible, even more daunting. Tanned, sculpted, mature. This was no teenager with whom she was exploring, no leftover New Uniform high-school fantasy come to life.

Damien Halliburton was all man.

And as he walked towards the bed, popping the button of his trousers, unzipping his fly, she felt a sudden need to scurry to the head of the bed, but instead grabbed a hold of a hunk of her angora throw and hung on tight lest she pass out from pure anticipation.

He stepped out of his trousers and his black silk boxers in one go until he was naked from the top of his dark head to the flats of his large feet. He was ready for her in every way possible. Veins stood out on his arms as though he was straining. His jaw was sharp and his lips tightly clenched. His erection was quite simply glorious. And rather than let her simply admire he just kept on coming.

She tore her T-shirt over her head and the moment his knee hit the bed she was reaching up and wrapping a hand behind his neck and drawing him down to her.

He held himself away, only just, but enough so that he wouldn't crush her with his heavy weight, while his mouth held back nothing, plundering hers with his tongue, until she felt deliciously bruised.

He lowered himself to her side so that he could free his hands. To caress her stomach, which quivered beneath his touch. To brush her hair from her neck before following through with an array of searing kisses. When he gently nudged aside the strap of her bra with the tip of his nose and scraped the very bottom of her neck his tenderness almost broke her.

'So you are a shoulder girl,' he murmured into her neck, before nipping lightly outwards until his teeth sank into the soft flesh just before her shoulder-bone.

Her head dropped back to the bed and she arched into him. 'Who knew?' she managed to say.

'Well, if that works, I wonder…' He reached behind her, unclipped her bra with one hand, slid it away, then threw it to the other side of the room. His eyes turned impossibly dark as they roamed over her breasts, which felt so very heavy against her chest.

'Which one first?' He lowered himself so that she could feel his hot breath whisper across her breasts. Her nipples hardened into tight peaks as she fought against the urge to grab him by the back of the head and pull him down to whichever breast was closest.

He went left, laying a row of kisses beneath until she could have cried out. His tongue darted out, leaving a trail of moisture until his mouth closed over her nipple. A spasm rocketed through her, lifting her hips off the bed.

He lightly grazed her with his teeth before moving over to the right breast and following the same pattern, which only made her ache more, knowing exactly what was coming next.

Once she was sure she could stand it no more, he began kissing down the sensitive inside of her arm. There was little she could do but let her arm hang limply in his care as wave after wave of warmth spilled outward from every touch of his mouth.

His hand trailed a gentle course along the beltline of her track pants, and then he blew across her naked stomach until a wave of agonising goose-bumps sprang up. Her hand flew to rub the skin prickles away but he stopped her.

'Uh-uh. This part is mine now.'

She lifted her head enough to catch his eye. 'Says who?'

'Says the guy who is about to show you why you should stop yabbering and just let him do as he pleases.'

As he spoke his fingers stroked back and forth across her stomach, moving ever lower with each caress, until they began to push her pants lower and lower past her hips.

Her neck muscles gave way, her head collapsed, and her arm flopped over her eyes until all she could see was the backs of her eyelids. All she could hear was the heavy sound of her own breath. And all she could feel was the smooth slide of velour down her thighs, past her calves and off.

The central heating was on low to hold the cold autumn afternoon at bay. But her skin felt as if it were on fire. As if she was blushing from head to foot. Her blood vessels must have been on overload.

The bed shifted as Damien moved. Her imagination went crazy as she tried to foresee what he would do next. And just as she thought she couldn't take the wait another second his hands closed around her feet.

His thumbs rubbed the soles, his fingers sliding against the muscles of her ankles until she sighed with the luscious pleasure of it. They moved up her calves, making her thank her lucky stars she'd shaved that morning. Once they hit her knees she began to shake. Her self-control broke down, inch by beautiful inch.

His caress was so gentle as his hands rounded her thighs, kneading ever so slightly before delving in between and pressing her legs until they fell apart. One hand continued up her side, his thumb brushing into her navel, then up her ribcage as he again rested beside her.

His mouth claimed hers in the very same instant his other hand reached the juncture between her thighs.

Her groan was swallowed by his insistent mouth, his searching tongue. She writhed beneath him, her senses confused as to whether to let her concentrate on the delicious sensation of his lips playing, oh, so gently, and, oh, so tenderly with hers, or to let go and give into the feel of his fingers touching her, stroking her, sliding against her flesh with ever so slightly increasing pressure and pace that her whole body thrummed.

She began to peak all too soon. She tilted her head sideways and begged him, 'Wait.'

'Not going to happen.' His gravelly voice almost sent her over the edge all on its own.

'I don't want this to end,' she said, her voice now a desperate whimper. But it was the truth. In her blissful state she could truly imagine holding back, slowing down, and finding a way to feel like this until the end of time.

'Too bad,' Damien said, then kissed her until she was completely breathless.

With that, she finally allowed herself to feel every ounce of pleasure. The kiss, the caress, the weight of him pressing against her came together as a slow boiling-point vibration coursing from her centre and spreading out through every nerve ending to the tips of her fingers and toes.

The hand over her eyes reached out and clung to his shoulder. Her right knee bent and spilled sideways until she was completely open to him, body and soul.

And the heat, and shakes, and pleasure and lack of control came to a head until her whole body went numb for one brief idyllic second before sensation returned and rolled through her like a tidal wave, destroying every shred of restraint in its wake, leaving her so ragged she had not even enough energy to lift a finger.

'Open your eyes,' Damien said an eon later. She struggled against the heavy weight of her eyelids before she was able to blink into the late afternoon light, which sent the cream walls in her room a bright burnt orange.

He looked deep into her eyes, and she was too shattered to hide what she felt for him. But what she saw in his eyes soon woke her up.

Burgeoning compassion. Genuine, honest to goodness care that he had in no way hurt her. Which meant that he believed he had the power within himself to do so. Which in turn meant that, not only was he arrogant as all get out, he also saw far more in her expression than she cared to reveal.

She broke eye contact, crossed her legs, lifted herself up onto her elbows and leaned up to kiss him, to run her tongue along his bottom lip before taking it between her teeth and tugging him until it must have hurt a little bit.

She reached out until she found the evidence of just how very turned on he still was. She looked up at him from beneath her eyelashes and said, 'Your turn.'

And the look in his eyes changed. Concern transformed into heat. Desire. Self-interest. That she could handle.

'Condom?' he asked, and she pointed to the top bedside drawer. He reached out with one long arm, found what he was looking for, tore the packet open with his teeth and was sheathed and ready to go before she even had the chance to take another breath.

And then he pulled her to him, kissing her with newfound intensity, crushing her against his broad chest, wrapping his leg around her until she felt so small in his arms. If he continued doing this to her, making her feel so powerful and vulnerable all at once, she was terrified she might start to cry.

So she gathered every vestige of strength she had and rolled him over until she was lying on top of him, one leg casually thrown across his.

At first his face registered surprise, but then the gleam in his eyes took on more light as a sinful smile spread across his face. He rolled onto his back until she lay fully atop him.

'Helpful as always,' she said.

He grinned, like the wolf just before he revealed himself as a villain to Little Red Riding Hood. 'Mmm. Though I don't know if there is a scout badge for my brand of helpfulness.'

She pushed herself into a sitting position, nudged herself against him until his eyes closed and his mouth fell open. 'Next time I find myself up close and personal with a scout leader I'll suggest it.'

His eyes flew open and his hands snuck out and grabbed her by the buttocks, stilling her, controlling her still even while he looked beyond ready to lose all control. 'It's not smart to tease me about being up close and personal with another man while I have you like this.'

'You don't have me,' she said. 'Not yet.'

She reached up and held her hot hair off her sweaty neck. Damien's eyes zeroed in on her breasts and glazed over. She lifted onto her knees, and he groaned. Then she sank down over him until her eyes fell closed with bliss.

And he began to rock. The rhythm so easy, so unhurried, she gave in and went along for the ride.

He ran his palm down her front, moulding her left breast, then running lovingly along each rib before landing across her hip, his thumb resting at the juncture of where their bodies met. And there it stayed. Seemingly accidental, but so erotic Chelsea found her desire building with such unexpected and sudden force she fell back and grabbed a hold of his thighs.

The change in position only made the pleasure all the greater. For her and for him. She saw it in the darkening of his eyes. The sweat beads on his brow. The tendons straining in his neck. She felt it in the grip on her hips, in the impossible deepening pressure inside her.

The rocking soon quickened. The heat between them scorching until she too was lathered in a layer of sweat. She could taste it on her upper lip. Feel it cruelly tickling every inch of her hot skin.

'Chelsea,' he called out and it was enough to loosen any last withholding place inside her. She let her head fall back, pressed her hips into his. She left just enough room for his thumb to slide between them and as though he could read her every move he did as he was told.

Her whole body throbbed. Ached. Needle-sharp stings pricked her all over as a draught washed across her damp skin.

Then everything changed as Damien swelled inside her, as his thighs clenched beneath her hands and a primal roar tore through the heated silence.

With that she too let go, every sensation shrinking to the point where their bodies met before exploding in a burst of stars behind her eyes.

And as she finally fell apart in his arms, her cheeks burned hot with sweat and carefully hidden tears.

CHAPTER TEN

DAMIEN lay beside Chelsea as again she slept.

The faded top sheet covered her body, revealing only her smooth creamy neck and her soft jaw hidden partially behind feathers of her caramel-coloured hair. He braced himself on one arm and reached out, brushing her hair from her cheek, letting it slide over his fingers, smooth as silk.

She moved beside him. The sheet over her lithe body slid and shifted and settled until one bare breast was naked to the night air.

He stared at it like a drowning man would stare at a lifebelt, fighting the overwhelming desire to reach out and run a hand down her side. To wake her. To take her again.

Instead he ran a fast hand over his unshaven jaw, abrading the skin on his palm. For as it turned out the events of the evening had done nothing to quell his desire for her. It had only made him want more.

She was on the verge of waking. He should go.

He'd known her, what, two days? Three? They'd crammed a hell of a lot of getting-to-know-you stuff into that time, but it certainly hadn't made him take some dramatic about-turn in his life. He'd been on the market for a fling and he'd found one. It would be cruel to allow Chelsea to hope she was dealing with any other kind of man, especially after what he'd seen in her eyes as she lay sated in his arms.

Gathering his will-power, he slid out of her bed, found his suit trousers draped over an upholstered chair in the corner. He pulled them on for the third day running, zipped up, left his top button undone, then sat in the chair and watched her for who knew how long until she stirred again, this time her eyes flickering open.

'Hi,' she said, her voice husky.

He clenched his hands together to stop himself from bolting back into bed with her and damning the consequences.

She half sat up, demurely taking the sheet with her, her creamy skin lit blue by the moonlight spilling through her gauzy curtains. 'Is everything okay?'

Okay? No, it was not okay. Everything was moving too fast. They were both getting in over their heads. If he saw her again he'd only continue half-heartedly and end up hurting her. Unless…

Unless he was completely honest right now. Unless the boundaries and limits were spelt out in absolute final detail. 'I want to see you again,' he blurted before he could change his mind.

Her eyes softened, darkened. 'So come get me.'

He stuck a fingernail into the palm of the other hand to keep himself grounded. 'Not yet,' he said, and her eyes widened enough that he knew she was now fully awake.

He took a deep breath, filling his lungs to bursting point before he said what he needed to say. 'Chelsea, when I told you earlier that I recently came out of a bad relationship, I should have made myself perfectly clear.'

She blinked up at him, so sweet, so undeserving of what he was about to ask of her.

'The relationship was fine. Bonnie and I dated, exclusively, for two and a half years. We lived together for the past several months. Her parents know my parents. Our work timetables meshed neatly. I thought everything was perfectly comfortable. Until a month ago she gave me an ultimatum. Marry her or leave. It took me less than half a second to decide.'

She watched him carefully for a few moments before saying, 'Please tell me you left.'

He laughed despite himself. She was such a trouper. But she also couldn't hide the deep breaths, which proved she wasn't as ignorant of what he was trying to tell her as she made out.

'I left,' he said. 'So fast she barely had time to call me a heartless bastard more than three times before I was out the door.'

'I don't blame her. Sounds like you acted like a total cad,' she said, flicking her hair over her shoulder in a move that was pure self-defence. 'So why are you telling me this now?'

'Because I came into this with no expectations and now, even if it does indeed make me a heartless bastard, after last night I know I'm not yet ready to walk away from you.'

At that a slight smile tugged at her cheeks, at her soft lips; he did his all to not lose himself there and dragged his eyes upwards.

'But one day I will walk away. It's my *modus operandi*. I'm being utterly honest when I tell you that I'm not built for anything lasting or exclusive. It's not in my genetic make-up. All I have to offer is good company when it suits us both and, I think we can agree, some pretty great sex.'

He let that last word hang on the air, hoping it might be the thing to sway her. It sure swayed him.

She didn't say anything. Didn't agree, or disagree. She didn't cry, or rant, or toss her hair and feign indifference. She just watched him, her eyes steady on his as she let his statement sink in.

'I could be making a total ass of myself,' he said, giving himself and her one last out, 'even bringing this up. You could well have been ready to tell me to sod off and never see you again. And if that's the case, I wouldn't blame you either.'

He felt enormous relief at having set the ground rules before this went any further. Though his lungs felt tighter and tighter with every passing second as he awaited her verdict.

Finally, she shifted, lifting herself upright until the sheet fell away, leaving her naked to the waist. Then she lifted the sheet for him, welcoming him back into her bed.

Weak sunlight tickled the backs of Chelsea's eyelids. A self-indulgent smile made its way across her face before she even opened her eyes.

She stretched her beautifully aching limbs and reached out to find the other side of the bed was empty. Cool. Ruffled to prove she hadn't dreamt the events of the night, but devoid of Damien all the same.

She slid her naked form from the bed and grabbed her gown before heading out of the bedroom only to discover the apartment was silent. There was no gorgeous dark-haired man sitting in the kitchen nook, no newspaper splayed out over her small table, no breakfast waiting for her.

She could picture such a scene so clearly it felt like more than a memory. Or a wish. But the reality she was given was that he wasn't there.

Which was fine. Really. Especially since the tenderness with which he'd made love to her when he'd come back to bed after his little speech had tempered the difficult words, and she'd fallen asleep assured that not kicking him out on his ear had been the right move.

She ignored the nagging, dissenting buzzing in her head as

she shuffled into the kitchen, where a white folded piece of paper lay atop the coffee percolator. He'd left her a note. A smile stretched across her face until she noticed the percolator was cold.

If she was to be consistent and continue with the 'actions speak louder than words' mantra she was clinging to, no matter what the note said the cold percolator told her something far more potent.

Damien had foregone his usual aromatic morning brew as he hadn't wanted to wake her. To face her. To kiss her goodbye.

The buzzing in her ears soon became a twisting in her heart as the enormity of what she'd agreed to bubbled over her.

She closed her eyes and clung to the kitchen bench. 'You daft mug. You know your feelings for the guy are already far too strong to accept something so casual. Of course kicking him out on his ear was what needed to be done. But, no, you just had to have him again.'

Her mobile rang and she was so tense she jumped in fright, the note crumpling in her palm.

She checked the number. It was him. She took a deep breath, put on her smoothest phone voice, and answered. 'Chelsea speaking.'

'Good morning, sunshine,' he said, his voice thick with suggestion.

Her uncooperative knees turned to jelly and she slumped against the kitchen bench, clutching her gown shut over her naked breasts, which were already straining as though they too were wondering why he wasn't still there.

'I'm taking you out tonight,' he said. 'I've seen how you react to a good feed.'

She tried desperately to find a way to give herself more time. Either to come to terms with his terms or to extricate herself from this thing without looking a complete fool. And in the end came up with, 'What if I'm busy? I might have a date with someone else.'

'So you'll cancel,' he insisted.

A shot of searing frustration jolted her upright. He was the one who wasn't making any promises about keeping his goods just for her, for goodness' sake. 'What if I don't want to cancel?'

'I…I don't quite know what to say to that.'

She could feel his own impatience pouring through the phone. And this time when she chose to pay more attention to his actions than to his words all she could see was his level of care, the look in his eye when he was about to kiss her, the fact that he regarded her highly enough to be so honest with her in the first place.

She slapped a hand over her forehead as she said, 'Oh, relax, Damien. I'm coming out with you.'

'Tease,' he said, the lingering hum in his voice telling her he liked it.

'Bossy boots,' she shot back. 'So where are we going?'

'A little Jamaican bar around the corner from my office we often go to after work. How do you like rum?'

She shrugged. 'Don't mind it.'

'And bars full of men in suits?'

'Love them to bits.'

'Mmm, I thought you might. So how about it? You, me, a hundred of my closest friends, a leather couch and a couple of rum toddies to keep us warm this cool autumn evening.'

Right, so he didn't want to be her boyfriend, but he didn't mind introducing her to the people in his life. As what? She ran her hand over her eyes.

'So what does one wear to a Jamaican pub to meet your closest friends?'

'Ah, I'd suggest not a lot of buttons. Or layers.'

Chelsea blinked, having had no idea that this season buttons must have been some kind of fashion *faux pas*.

'So long as it's easy for me to take off,' he clarified, and her tension didn't subside one little bit. It only morphed all too easily into a flurry of imaginings about him sliding a dress over her head versus tugging trousers over her thighs.

I can do this, she thought. *I'm strong. I can put up with a lot to have more of this man.*

'I'll pick you up around eight,' he said.

She nodded.

He laughed. 'Have a good day, Chelsea.' Then he hung up.

Chelsea put the phone down, and realised she still had his note crunched up in her hot palm. She unfurled it.

'Early meeting,' it read. 'Seriously. I'll call you. D.'

With a growl she tossed it into the sink where a few drops of moisture made the blue writing bleed.

That evening Chelsea sat on a backless barstool, trying to keep her back straight, and running her finger back and forth through a drop of condensation that had slithered from the glass of her Jamaican Cobbler to the shiny black bar.

It had been a long day. She'd had to contend with a phone call from Kensey, who'd pressed and pressed until Chelsea had filled her in on as much of her past couple of days as she could while keeping the conversation clean. Another from *Chic* magazine, pushing her interview up a week. And yet another from the bank manager wondering if she'd signed the papers as yet.

All the while she'd managed to find plenty of time in her over-packed day to go over every second of her relationship with Damien all the way up until he'd had to sit her down and give her *the talk*.

She could feel a tension headache coming on.

She glanced over her shoulder to look for Damien, who had disappeared to find a quiet corner amongst the fake palm trees less than five minutes earlier when his mobile had rung.

But all she could see apart from the blinding green black and yellow décor of the up-market city bar was a sea of New Uniform types. All grown up yet no less sure of themselves and their privileged place in the world. She was pretty sure Damien would never have made a speech like the one he had to any one of the glossy nymphettes gyrating on the dance floor. He wouldn't have needed to. As they skimmed their hands over one young guy after another they looked as if they understood the transitory nature of affection.

Thankfully his 'friends' hadn't arrived as yet so she hadn't had to try to be whatever he introduced her to them as being.

'So sorry,' Damien said as he came from nowhere to slide onto the seat beside hers. 'My father after his weekly report.'

Chelsea raised what she hoped might be a sophisticated eyebrow. 'You're a little old for that, don't you think?'

'He's retired. Bored out of his mind. Mum has a bunch of cronies over for drinks every Friday night and I think I'm his way of feeling like he's still out there climbing the corporate ladder rather than spending his days following my mother around like a good little lapdog.'

'Yet they're divorced.'

'That they are. And so much happier that way. No strings. Meaning they can do whatever they please when they please. They just so happen to be pleased with one another at the moment.'

He grinned at the idea. He actually grinned. As though he thought she was so on the same page as him about those nutty types who thought marriage and commitment were something to aim for, she'd feel the overwhelming need to grin back.

She rubbed at her now throbbing temple.

'And speaking of dear old Dad, he has some experience in banking too, you know,' he said. 'I'm sure he'd be prepared to look over your loan papers if you'd like him to. He'd be able to spot any dodgy loopholes in an instant and it would make him feel like he still has his finger on the pulse.'

She continued staring at Damien as though she'd never seen him before. He was willing to introduce her to his friends and his parents even though he wasn't willing to promise he would ever be there when she woke up in the morning. She would never inflict any guy on Kensey and her family unless it was serious.

'I'm not yet sure I'm even going to go that way,' she said.

'Why on earth not?'

She closed her eyes for a second and reminded herself *never* to let Kensey anywhere near him, no matter how long they stayed together. She'd never be allowed to make a decision on her own.

She opened her eyes to be blinded by the kaleidoscope of colour shining from the mirrored wall behind the bar. The drum-heavy music now pulsated inside her head. And she thought, *Well, if you can't beat 'em…*

'Do you want to dance?' she asked.

Damien looked at her as if she'd grown an extra head, but when the dance song eased into a slow and ultra-romantic beat, he put his untouched drink down, gave the barman a wink, then took her hand and eased her through the crowd out onto the dance floor.

Half a dozen women gave him the eye before giving her a once-over. In her tight jeans and black off-the-shoulder top she felt as if she ought to have at least looked like she belonged. Still she grabbed his hand tighter.

He spun her out and then into his arms until he held her in the classic ballroom hold. She had to look up to see into his eyes, which were smiling down at her. Pristine pools of blue.

The lights turned low, with only sporadic shafts of disco-ball light flickering over his face, proving his eyes never left hers.

The words of the song permeated. Talking of fear and tears and not knowing whether to hang on tight or go back to being lonely and confused. She leant her head on his shoulder and blocked them out.

As they slowly moved around the hardwood floor she felt their bodies meld closer together of their own accord. She managed to slide inside the soft lining of his suit jacket until her stomach rested flush against his with only two swathes of thin cotton separating her building warmth from his.

There, she thought, her whole body sighing in relief. In his arms everything felt okay. Better. As if she weren't a fool agreeing to his terms even though she knew she was a thousand miles further down the road towards wanting this to last for ever than he was.

Whether he leaned down or she stood on tiptoe first, she had no idea. Their lips met, gentle yet insistent. Her eyes closed and she drank him in.

His kiss was like magic, pouring warmth and unstoppered emotion through her body until she reached up and ran her hands around his neck, clinging to him, impressing herself upon him in every way possible.

His tongue lapped the roof of her mouth, sending her into some kind of free fall. She tipped her head to the side and opened her mouth to him, and with it her whole heart.

He let go of her hand and reached down to cup her buttocks, pushing her against the evidence of just how turned on he was.

'Not here,' she said against his mouth.

His eyes flickered open, dark and heavy with desire. She would have put money on the fact he hadn't even remembered where they were. She was momentarily tormented by the fact at times he was so sure, so clear-headed, and other times keeping his hands off her seemed more than he could bear.

'Where?' he said.

'Let's get out of here.' She dragged him from the dance floor, through the heaving, glittery crowd.

'But we haven't had dinner.'

'I don't need a feed to put me in the right mood.'

'So it would seem.' Damien had found his head after all. He moved in tight behind her as he hastily collected their things from the cloakroom, nodded a quick goodbye to the bouncer and herded her out into the chill evening air. She shivered; he gathered her close.

They scooted around the corner into the car park, and Damien was off driving down the street towards Chelsea's apartment before she'd strapped herself in.

She leaned back against the leather headrest in the passenger seat of Damien's gorgeous primrose-yellow Austin-Healey Sprite. The top was down, her hair was flying, she felt just fabulous, as if every drudging daily concern had been whipped out of her ears to be lost on the wind.

This was the life. The kind of life she could be living hanging with the likes of Damien Halliburton of the Halliburton Halliburtons. This was the fire, electricity, excitement, danger, no care for the consequences she'd *known* he had to offer before she'd even known his name.

'Where can I get me one of these?' she yelled.

'One of what?'

'This car. Tell me they go for a song. Please.'

'More like an opera than a song.'

Damien glanced sideways and offered her a sexy smile. Their eyes locked and held. She couldn't wait to get back to her place and knew he couldn't either.

'Hang on,' he said. Dragging the car down into such a low gear it groaned, he turned off the main road and headed towards the Docklands precinct with its wide open spaces cleared for future high-rise developments and phenomenal view of the Melbourne city skyline.

The second the car pulled to a stop atop a patch of grass hidden behind a billboard they were in one another's arms.

They came together with such force, such unbridled passion, it was as though they'd been away from one another's touch for years, not mere minutes.

Fast and furious, she thought. Then right on top of that... *It can't last for ever.* For Damien the relationship would burn out, or she would from the sheer force of keeping her true feelings from him.

Blocking out her contrary thoughts, Chelsea was in Damien's lap and he'd flipped the seat back as far as it would go. In that moment she regretted wearing jeans. She wanted him so desperately. Needed to lose herself in the sensations he created in her to stop the torrent of rebellious emotion sweeping over her.

He groaned. 'I haven't done this since I was a teenager. I only hope I'm still as flexible.'

'If you're not, I am,' she said, and his next groan was lost in her kiss.

He was right, she thought five minutes later when both of their shirts had been tossed into the back seat. They sure could make some beautiful love together.

So how could he be so wrong about the rest?

Her eyes flew open, and she was momentarily shocked by

the sight of the Melbourne skyline looming huge and glittering before her. The sky was black and clear, the moon large and luminous lighting the glossy dew on the grass around the car. She shivered.

'You can't be cold,' Damien said, wrapping his arms about her and pulling her to him. Her breasts scraped against the hair on his chest as he only added to her physical pleasure by biting into that magical spot where her neck met her shoulder.

But even that wasn't enough to cover up the certainty that none of it was enough. And never would be. She was in love with him. She wanted a future with him. What she didn't want was to see him day in and day out knowing it was only one step closer to the time she'd have to say goodbye.

'Stop,' she whispered, but her throat caught the word before it made it to the outside world. So with greater force she said, 'Damien, no more.' And she pushed him away.

'Are you all right?' he asked, his voice barely more than a rumble. 'Did I hurt you?'

She sat up, her eyes frantically searching the back seat for her bra, her top, anything to make her feel less painfully naked. She slid her top over herself, inside out though it was. And had to swipe a tear that she felt sliding from her left eye.

She pulled herself off his lap and he helped her, running his hands down her arms as though checking for broken bones. He glanced up into her eyes and must have seen the anguish therein as he swallowed, and his own eyes were suddenly filled with such care it made her choke.

'Chelsea, what did I do?'

'Nothing,' she blabbed. 'Truly. It's me. All me. I just…' God, how could she say this without sounding ridiculous, and giving herself away completely? 'This affair, or whatever it is we have going on, I don't think I can do it.'

Damien leaned slowly back into his seat and ran a hand through his hair. 'But last night... I thought we'd agreed it was what we both wanted.'

'I know, I did. I thought I did. But as it turns out I can't.'

'So in the past twenty-four hours what's changed?

I've fallen in love with you, you idiot!

'I've changed my mind. It's a woman's prerogative.'

He swore loud enough it seemed to echo across the large empty block of land. He reached into the back seat of the car and grabbed his shirt and jacket, tugging them over his arms as her words sank in. And when he spoke again his voice was deathly quiet. 'I never promised you anything.'

'I know.' Hers was barely above a whisper.

'So this is it. You're breaking up with me?'

God, was she really?

'What difference does it make?' she asked, prolonging the final step. 'You said it yourself, there will be an end point. I just think it would be better to end it now.'

'I don't agree.'

Did he have to make it so hard? Couldn't he see her heart was breaking for him? In that moment she so wanted to reach out and beat her hands on his chest until he could see the truth. Instead her anger turned to words.

Her voice was chilly when she said, 'The last thing I need in my life is another man who is going to let me down.'

His chest swelled as he took the barbs full on. 'And the last thing I need in my life is another woman making demands of me I simply can't fulfil.'

Chelsea crossed her arms over her chest as she realised she had begun to shiver for real. 'Well, then, you should be thanking me for letting you off the hook.'

He ran his hand over his face and with it seemed to wipe

away every ounce of feeling. 'I can't believe I'm saying this, but I should have listened to Caleb.'

'About what? About me?' Her accompanying laughter was shrill. 'Not bright and shiny enough for his tastes? Well, you can tell him I don't think much of him either.'

Finally, he looked at her. His eyes were so dark, so hooded in the moonlight she had no idea what he was thinking. 'You don't even know him.'

'I know enough to guess he wouldn't be thrilled with the idea of you slumming it with someone who clips dogs' toenails for a crust.'

Damien's laughter was tinged with a bitterness she hadn't imagined he might possess. 'God, Chelsea, I have never met a woman with as big a chip on her shoulder as you have.'

His tone only made her more sure. And more angry. With him, and with herself for ever thinking he might be different. He might be worth putting her defenceless heart on the line for.

'Well, don't panic,' she spat out, 'you won't have to worry about your friend's anxiety for your well-being any more. You and he can go off to some other swanky club with your bright and shiny friends and talk money and markets and boating and tennis, because I have a glorious weekend mapped out for me where I belong. In a dilapidated cabin in the Yarra Valley with my sister, her balding husband, their nutty three kids, and goofy dog, eating cheese on toast, crowded around the twelve-inch television, playing Pass the Parcel at a six-year-old's birthday party. Your scene's not my scene and vice versa. And I say thank goodness for that.'

She stopped to take a breath. Her lungs felt tight, her cheeks hot, even in the cold evening air.

'Are you done?' he asked, his voice cool.

She gathered every ounce of self-preservation she had inside her, turned to him and said, 'Even better. We're done, Damien. So are you going to take me home now or do I have to hitch-hike?'

He looked at her for several long seconds. She was close enough she could see every single hair on his head as the breeze lifted it off his face, see the twitching of a muscle in his left cheek, the rise and fall of his breaths beneath his quickly buttoned shirt.

And with every passing second she felt him moving further and further away, taking with him any warmth and hope she'd ever felt in her heart.

He licked his lips, shucked his jacket into a more comfortable position, then turned over the engine with a steady hand.

This time as he drove her through the dark city streets he kept just below the speed limit. Already there was nothing between them bar space and time, and the wind whipping about her face only served to take away her tears.

As he pulled up at the end of Flinders Lane, Chelsea turned to him to…what? Apologise? Wish him well? Change her mind? Beg him to love her back?

But he kept his gaze dead ahead, his fingers clenched hard to the steering wheel, his jaw set like stone.

She slid from the car, grabbed her jacket and bag from the back seat, and had barely closed the door when his engine gunned and he was gone down the glistening city street until she had nothing but the sound of his revving engine to prove he'd ever even been there.

For a moment she felt a bond with the faceless Bonnie. She felt the pain that woman must have felt at having to watch this man slip through her fingers. Chelsea tried to console herself with the fact that she hadn't lost two and a half years of her life before coming to the realisation that the man couldn't be tamed.

But she wouldn't worry any more about his past. For her future felt as bright and rosy and full of possibilities as the gutter beneath her feet.

CHAPTER ELEVEN

MID Saturday afternoon Damien was sitting on a large brown leather ottoman at the rear of Caleb's favourite haunt, a dapper mirror-and-wood-infested bar tucked away secretly beneath Russell Street.

He'd been staring blindly at the half-melted ice cubes clinking around the bottom of his untouched Scotch for goodness knew how long when a familiar scent tickled at his nose. Something warm, and soft and homey.

He glanced up, enough of him expecting to find a beautiful caramel-blonde walking towards him that his skin warmed a degree and the hairs on the back of his neck rose.

But instead all he saw was a slick redhead passing for at least the third time that hour. She caught his eye, and he smiled. She was gorgeous, she deserved recognition and that was what he was here to do. To mingle with the plethora of gorgeous young things on offer. To move on from Chelsea London, who herself had been meant to mean no more to him than a scratch for his itch.

The redhead pulled up to supposedly fix her shoe and held eye contact, brazen as you like. He knew all it would take was a tilt of his head, a broadening of his smile, to bring her over, to begin the dance, but at the last second he looked away.

'Since when did you become such a grumpy old man?' Caleb asked as he threw himself onto the ottoman until he was lazing across it like some modern day Caligula.

Damien sniffed in deep, letting the scents of all the mixed perfumes, wash away all memory of Chelsea's scent for good. 'Since the day you came into my life and I realised I was to become an unpaid babysitter until my dying day.'

'Funny. You know that redhead's been giving you eye all afternoon.'

'So she has.' Damien brought his drink to his lips.

'But she's no hottie dog groomer, is she?'

Damien's hand stilled, the smell of Scotch in his nose, the taste of it still missing from his lips. 'I wouldn't know,' he said. 'She may well be.'

'You really like this girl, don't you?'

'I liked her well enough.' Damien didn't even pretend to not know to whom Caleb was referring. He licked his bottom lip and nodded, squinting out into the hazy room rather than looking Caleb in the eye, rather than giving away just how much he'd liked her.

'Then what the hell are you doing sitting here moping with me when you could be elbow-deep in all that lovely warm, willing female flesh?'

'That particular female flesh is not so willing any more.'

'That was quick. What happened?'

'I was honest with her.'

Caleb sucked a hiss of air through his teeth. 'Bad move. What did you say?'

'I told her I couldn't give her any more than what we had.'

'And what was that exactly?'

Damien opened his mouth to say fun and games, but he knew that was rubbish. He searched for the words to describe what he and Chelsea had found together. To pinpoint what it was about her that made it so easy for him to reject it out of hand. And he couldn't. His mind felt bruised, making him unable to think straight about a lot of things.

'I made it clear we ought to keep things casual. Knowing neither of us was in a place to promise more. It's been a month since Bonnie, and Chelsea's, well, she's bloody neurotic.'

'And what did she have to say about that?'

'I thought… She thought… She told me where I could stick my offer.' With that he brought his Scotch to his mouth and let its watered down bitterness sear his throat.

Then behind the resultant hum in his ears he heard Caleb laugh. So loud and so hard the ottoman began to shake. He turned to his friend and glared.

But Caleb just grinned back. 'You poor devil.'

'Excuse me?'

Caleb sat up, rested a hand upon his shoulder, looked him in the eye and said, 'I'm thinking the hot get-back-on-the-horse cat lady has turned out to be the one.'

He waited for the punchline. For the jibe. But it never came. Caleb instead looked, if anything, envious.

'The one what?' Damien asked.

Caleb took a deep breath and seemed to search for patience. 'When you left Bonnie, you never sought to drown your sorrows in a glass of Scotch. But since you met this girl, you've been distracted, you've been moody, you've been a right dullard socially. And it's all because you've gone and accidentally found yourself the one woman in the world who was finally able to capture your imagination enough to pull you from the world of boring bliss in which we found ourselves born.'

It took about thirty seconds for Caleb's words to stop echoing inside Damien's head. 'You're dead wrong, mate. One woman, marriage, house and home... I can't. If being a Halliburton taught me anything—'

'Don't go holding up your crazy parents as some kind of example, my friend. They're madly in love and both half sloshed before dinner. And if it wasn't for the number their divorce did on the two of you I would have run off with your sister years ago.'

Damien kept his mouth shut and let Caleb's words sink in. Chelsea. The one. His *sister?*

'You and Ava?'

Caleb smiled, though there was no roguish humour in his eyes. 'We're focussing on you right now, my friend.'

'Right. Me. And Chelsea.' *The one.*

He'd told her he didn't want permanence, or exclusivity, because he'd thought he couldn't give them. He hadn't wanted to hurt her because he'd seen the way she was falling for him. But the truth was, he'd pulled back because he'd been falling for her too. And from what he'd learnt about her dating history, and her childhood, he knew she was just as jittery about the prospect of for ever as he was. And having never been in that predicament in his whole life he'd been trying his hardest to stop himself from getting hurt too.

When all the while she'd been there, offering herself. Offering a whole new world.

'I'm a bloody fool.'

'Nah, you're just a man. But you're also a Halliburton man and Halliburton men have a knack for getting everything they always wanted. So how about you stop cramping my style and get the hell out of here and go find your girl and get down on your knees and beg her to forgive you for being such a prat?'

Damien's mind swirled so fast he could barely focus. 'Don't you need a lift home?'

'Damien. Leave now, before I stick a boot in your butt for making me feel so syrupy sweet I might puke.'

Caleb stood then and reached out to take Damien's hand, helping him stand. At the last moment they hugged, in a manly fashion, thumping fists on one another's backs. But it was enough for Damien to know that Caleb wasn't entirely the blackguard he made himself out to be.

He too was a man content enough on the island to himself, but who would give away every speck of sand if it meant truly finding the woman he could love for ever.

As he pushed blindly past transient, easy men and women that until now he'd always thought just like him to get to the front door, to fresh air and sunshine he so desperately craved, he patted his pockets for his car keys, his mobile phone.

They were all he needed where he was going. That and a whole lot of luck on his side.

Chelsea sat on a swinging love seat on the front porch of the ramshackle wooden house that Kensey and Greg had bought with the money she'd paid them for Kensey's half of the apartment. Kids' bikes lay forgotten on the patchy lawn beside her Pride & Groom van. Hanging plants made a jungle of the roof above her.

She'd rolled her mobile over and over in her hands so many times it was warm to the touch. Not that she wanted to call anyone. It just made her feel connected to the world she'd left behind in the city.

'That's the last thing you need,' she said aloud as she shoved it into the back pocket of her faded jeans.

She'd signed the bank-loan papers and sent them off. She'd put Phyllis completely in charge at the salon for the day. She'd made the beginnings of what would be many changes to her life to give herself the illusion she had it back under her control.

Now what she needed was fresh air, space, new scenery. And this was the place for it. This place that felt more like home than any other she'd ever known. It was true. Real. Messy. Honest. Unpretentious. And the complete opposite of Damien Halliburton's world of fast and furious bright and shiny living. If she had to pick one place in the world to lick her wounds and get over him, and to get over the trust she'd so naively put into the possibility of him, this was it.

Suddenly Hurley kids galore spilled out of every available doorway fracturing the peace. 'Auntie Chelsea!' one said. 'Have you seen my Spiderman pyjamas?'

Another asked, 'Can you give me a piggyback?

'What did you bring me for my birthday?' said the third.

'Ah, no, later and that's a surprise,' she said, giving each of them a quick kiss before they were gone around the side of the house as quickly as they'd arrived.

Kensey came out of the kitchen wiping her hands on a tea towel.

'My sister, the little woman,' Chelsea said, moving over to make space for her.

Kensey sat. 'Are you ever coming inside?'

A gust of wind swirled a pile of autumn leaves down the dirt driveway. 'In a minute.'

'It's getting cool. Dinner will be ready in forty odd minutes. And the kids keep asking why you're frowning.'

Knowing she could never fool Kensey as well as she could fool herself, Chelsea dropped her head into her hands and frowned to her heart's content. She revelled in it, feeling as sorry for herself as she wanted. 'I'm frowning because I'm miserable,' she sulked.

'Of course you are. But good riddance to bad rubbish, I say. Who needs a handsome, hunky, rich guy who cooks and isn't scared of a little illness lusting after them? You did the right thing cutting him off. Feel better?'

Chelsea lifted her head and somehow managed to laugh. 'Infinitely,' she lied. 'Thanks ever so much for your understanding.'

'He did make you glow, though, pet.'

'Kensey—' she warned.

'Well, he did. Made you glow and glisten and act all gooey and girly and give me hope that one day I'll be able to get you off my hands for good.'

'If you truly do want to get me off your hands for good, then you'd do better than to say things like that while I'm in the process of moving on.'

Kensey drew her in for a hug. 'You're right. Sorry. You will feel better. Eventually. Time wounds all heals and all that. And until then, tonight…there's cake. And vodka. And a Hugh Jackman movie marathon on the telly.'

'Thank goodness for you,' Chelsea said, feeling some small measure of relief that her itinerant father and absentee mother had given her this woman in her life at least. Everything else would come together eventually. Her business, her love life, her broken heart.

Hopefully.

The sudden grumble of a high-octane engine had them facing the road. When Chelsea saw Damien's sports car pull into the driveway she had to blink twice to make sure she hadn't conjured him up from her gloomy imaginings.

'Holy cow,' Chelsea said.

'Lookie here,' Kensey said.

'Nice wheels,' Greg said, coming outside to see what the noise was about. 'Who's that?'

'*That* would be Chelsea's Damien,' Kensey said.

'Ooh,' Greg said. 'He's flash, Chels. Handsome fella too. So why did you dump him again?'

Kensey answered for her. 'I believe the theory on this one was do unto others before they do unto you.'

Chelsea heard their words as though they were coming from the other side of the world. Despite having let him go, seeing him again in the flesh had every part of her straining towards the car, and the man getting out of it.

The man in the sleek black suit, the crisp baby-blue shirt, the silk tie that likely cost more than her whole outfit, with the dark preppy hair lifting sexily in the breeze. The man she'd watched drive away only the night before, certain she'd never see him again. The man who was behind the fact that she now sat there with unwashed hair, red-rimmed eyes and an aching chest.

'Kensey, do you know anything about this?' she whispered loudly, but Kensey just shrugged, and snuck towards Greg, who put an unconscious arm around her waist. 'Then how on earth did he find me?'

And more importantly, why?

Damien shut the door, straightened his jacket, then turned and found the three of them watching him. He lifted his hand to give a short wave, then let it drop.

Chelsea motioned with her eyes for Kensey and Greg to make themselves scarce, but Kensey just smiled all the bigger.

Damien slid his keys into his trouser pocket and headed up the path. He ran a hand through his hair. She'd never seen him looking so nervous before. Or so adorable. And completely out of place in the rustic setting as she'd known he would be.

But he was there. And that was something.

She suddenly didn't know what to do with her hands. To wring them, cross her arms, or slide them into the back pockets of her jeans. In the end she let them hang at her sides in loose fists.

Damien stopped at the foot of the steps and looked up at her. His blue eyes so achingly familiar and beautiful they managed to create a new series of cracks in her already fragmented heart.

'What are you doing here, Damien?' She was dead pleased when her voice came out without shaking.

His mouth curved into a half-smile and he said, 'I was passing through. You know there's a wine-tasting festival down the road?'

Well... Her eyebrows shot skyward and she had a whole slew of retorts to shoot back at him despite the audience before he held up a hand, shook his head and pinned her with the most serious gaze she'd ever seen him use.

'Wipe that last statement. Please,' he said. 'I drove up here without really knowing what I would say when I got here. So let me start again.'

She shrugged.

His lungs filled and deflated before he said, 'I'm here to see you.'

Her heart rate kicked up a notch. Her long since empty well of hope filled so fast it threatened to spill over. But she couldn't let him see. He *hadn't* said he felt any differently than he had twenty-four hours before. 'How on earth did you find me?'

'I looked your sister up in the phone directory of a public phone booth in town.' He glanced at Kensey and nodded. 'A paper one. Sometimes technology isn't all it's cracked up to be.'

'You won't find any fancy technology here,' Greg said. 'Damien, right? I'm Greg Hurley and this is my wife Kensey.'

Thus invited, Damien sidled up the stairs, stopping at Chelsea's side.

'Chelsea's told me a lot about both of you,' he said.

She felt his warmth, smelled the faint rays of autumn sunshine clinging to his clothes as though loath to let go. She closed her eyes and leaned as far away from him and his magnetic scent as she could.

Then the Hurleys' collie chose that exact moment to bolt around the side of the house, run straight to the newcomer and leap, his great muddy paws landing smack bang in the centre of Damien's shirt.

'Oh, Lord. Slimer, down!' Kensey cried out.

Chelsea grabbed the dog by the collar, but he lived up to his name and slobbered all over her hand.

'He's fine,' Damien said, rubbing hard hands over the dog's ears and grinning from ear to ear. 'Slimer?' he said to Kensey. '*Ghostbusters* fans?'

Kensey's face broke into a matching grin. 'You bet. The reason I went out with Greg in the first place was because he reminded me of a young Bill Murray. Do you have a dog?'

He laughed. 'What's with you girls and dogs? Chelsea asked me the same thing on our first date.'

Chelsea felt as if she were in the twilight zone. She was so confounded she wasn't quick enough to stop Kensey from telling her tale.

'When we were little we spent a few months living out this way with a friend of our dad's. He was nice. His house was clean. He could cook. Which made me fall in love with him as only a hungry eight-year-old can. But for Chelsea it was all about his dog. A fluffy grey mongrel of a thing that only ate what we ate. That always looked and smelled worse five minutes after a bath. And who slept on the end of Chelsea's bed and followed her around like he was her guardian angel. She's had a thing for dogs, and the people who value them, ever since.'

Damien continued rubbing Slimer behind the ear, but his gaze was all for Chelsea. It was a nice gaze. A warm gaze. A gaze full of promise that he'd assured her again and again was not there. Glutton for punishment that she was, she gazed right on back. She needed her head read.

'But you've never owned a dog yourself?' he asked.

Chelsea shook her head.

'Yet you run a pet-grooming company?'

She narrowed her eyes and nodded, daring him to make something of it. To overstep the mark even slightly so that she could grab him by the scruff of the neck and shove him back into his car and out of her life, before all this niceness and dog-patting made her love him so much more she'd never *ever* get over him.

'When we eventually moved out of the place,' Kensey added to be that much more helpful, 'it was like the world had ended. Having to leave the dog behind broke poor Chelsea's heart. And I don't think she's ever found herself a replacement love who measured up with Rover's level of commitment and adoration.'

'Fascinating,' Damien said, slowly easing Slimer to four feet. He stood, blinked at Chelsea and she could see the wheels turning behind his far too intelligent blue eyes. 'Can we talk?'

Here we go. Without preamble she demanded of Kensey and Greg, 'You guys. Inside now.'

'Right,' Greg said, practically dragging Kensey away. 'Dinner's in half an hour.' Chelsea thanked her lucky stars he was smart enough to know if he'd extended an invitation to Damien she would have killed him.

Feeling far too close to Damien for comfort, Chelsea jogged down the stairs and headed around the side of the house towards the back yard. Damien followed close enough his smooth aftershave curled around her nostrils, blanketing the scent of Italian herbs and lemon cake wafting through the open windows.

'They seem nice,' he said.

'They are. And they mean everything to me. Whatever your reason for coming to find me, choosing to do so while I'm here is playing dirty. So say whatever you've come to say and make it quick. You heard Greg—I have less than half an hour before the macaroni and cheese is on.'

He shot her a quick sideways glance, which still told her nothing of his motives. Or of his opinion of macaroni and cheese. He could have been there because she'd left him in such a state the night before he'd come in the hopes for one last booty call, to prove to his ego that he could still have her despite her protestations, or for such fantastical reasons she dared not think for all the damage they could do to her determination to stop loving him.

She led him out to the back deck and folded her arms across the split-wood banister looking out over rolling hills covered in the spoils of other people's wealth. There were white grapes as far as the eye could see and a lone bright yellow hot-air balloon floated lazily across the sharp blue sky.

About a foot of space lay between her fingers and his. But he might as well have been leaning his might and muscle against her for the way he affected her simply by being near.

'It is beautiful here,' Damien said.

'Too quiet for your tastes, I would have thought.'

'Not at all.' A smile curved Damien's cheek and for a moment Chelsea forgot she was no longer allowed to lean in and kiss the crease at the edge of his mouth. To tuck herself against his side and take his arm and wrap it around her shoulders so that she could lean into all that strength and warmth.

She looked away, and she hoped he had not seen her intimate desires splashed across her face.

'If I wasn't here I'd be back in the city at a bar with Caleb.'

'Very cosmopolitan.'

'It was,' he said. 'A bunch of people I've never met and likely will never meet again, a glass of over-iced Scotch at my fingertips, and shouting at Caleb to be heard over the loud music.'

'Sounds just your kind of place,' she said.

'A week ago I would have said the same.'

She felt his eyes on her still, and she did her very best to hide the quickening inside her as she tried to decipher just what he was trying to say.

He turned to rest the backs of his elbows on the railing and crossed his feet at the ankles. Without the distraction of rolling hills of wheat-yellow grape vines laid out before him, his eyes were all for her.

Her eyes hurt from crying, her hair needed a brush, her nose was pink and her lips were raw from biting at them. While the late-afternoon sun lent his skin a glow that made him look so healthy it just wasn't fair.

But the way he looked at her...it was as if he couldn't even tell she looked a mess.

This time her voice shook like crazy as she asked, 'What are you doing here, Damien?'

CHAPTER TWELVE

DAMIEN reached out and pushed a lock of hair from Chelsea's cheek. The gentle touch did such things to her senses she gripped tighter to the railing to stop from trembling all over.

'I couldn't handle leaving things as we did,' he said.

She swallowed. 'It was pretty awful. But you didn't have to follow me out here to remind me. I think you know my mobile number.'

He smiled but it didn't really reach his eyes. 'Nevertheless I didn't want to tell you the things I have to say over the phone.'

She wished he had. Because then she could have cried silently while he broke things off in a more civilised way. Now she had to see him, smell him, hold herself together within touching distance of him.

'There's nothing more you need to say, Damien. Don't think walking away from this makes you the bad guy again. I understand where you are coming from. I do. But you meant what you said, and I meant what I said. So that's that. It was pretty great while it lasted, but now we *are* done.'

He nodded, though all the while his gaze still roved over her face as if he couldn't believe she was really there in front of him. And then he had to go and say, 'Then why did I miss you so terribly when I fell asleep last night? And when I woke up this morning. And as I drove up here breaking the land-speed record.'

No, no, no! the voices of reason inside her head screamed. *Don't do this to me!*

'When two people agree to stop seeing one another that's one of the down points,' she said.

'If you could tell me any up points to us not seeing one another, I'd like to hear them. Because I've racked my brain and I can't think of one.'

She shook her head. Hard enough to make her brain rattle and crash against the sides of her skull in punishment for momentarily agreeing with him. 'Damien, you were right to put the brakes on, and I was right to end it. Can't we just leave it at that?'

'Remind me why.'

She clenched her fists and dug her toes into the flaky mossy tiles beneath her feet and reminded herself he was smooth and gorgeous and always said the right things and that was why she'd fallen in love with him. But that it didn't mean he would ever love her back.

'Because,' she said, 'ninety per cent of the time you'll find me with limp hair, wet clothes, and head-to-toe sweat. I don't own a suit and you live in a world peopled by them. I eat leftovers for breakfast, not eggs hollandaise. My idea of a fabulous Saturday night is hunkered beneath a mohair blanket watching a movie in the park. I don't know one wine from another, I don't give a hoot about the FTSE or the yen, or bar openings, and when it comes down to it we don't have one single thing in common.'

'I think we've verified that we both love dogs,' he said, his voice so warm, so understanding, so near.

'Not good enough,' she said, squeezing her eyes shut.

'Okay, so I like movies. And mohair. And the idea of you in a wet T-shirt almost short-circuited my brain right now.'

At his words she actually felt her uncooperative breasts straining against the cotton of her long-sleeved T-shirt. 'I have no boobs. Wetting them is not exciting.'

'It's exciting to me.'

Damn him, he knew just how to get beneath her defences. She took a deep breath and mentally brought in reinforcements in the form of her old friends doubt and mistrust.

He reached out again and continued to play with her hair, sliding it over her back, running his fingers along that special place between her neck and shoulder. 'Chelsea, all I see every day are women in suits. Slick and cunning in head-to-toe Melbourne black. While you have been like a breath of fresh air in my life. Since the first moment I laid eyes on you it was like my world view shifted. No woman had ever sassed me like you did. No woman ever continually confounded me as you have. And no woman ever gave into me with as much delight as you did. And I find I can't let that go. I want you to come back to me. I want you to give us another chance.'

There. He'd said it. The words she ached for yet had hoped for the sake of her tender heart he hadn't come here to say.

'I couldn't,' she blurted out before she threw herself into his arms. 'I can't.'

'Why?' He moved nearer, all but blocking out the setting sun with his broad shoulders.

'Because *you* are one of those slick and cunning types in your head-to-toe Melbourne black.'

His languorous, sensual exploration of the skin behind her ear came to an agonising halt. It was obvious that was not the answer Damien had been expecting. 'Meaning?'

She momentarily blinked into his eyes before looking back

the ramshackle house with its broken roof tiles and faded
oral curtains. The real home and family her sister had built
r herself from the ashes of a debilitating childhood. A youth
ppered by parasitic—

'Men in suits,' she said aloud, 'from my experience, may
ver think to steal your wallet but would con the contents of
ur bank account out from under you as soon as look at you
it might make them an extra buck.'

'Is that really who you think I am?' he asked.

No, she thought instantly. But instead out of her mouth came
e words, 'I don't know who you are.'

A lock of hair fell across her face. She knew he'd noticed
t he didn't make a move to tuck it anywhere, so she was
rced to do so herself. But that was nothing compared with the
he that slammed her body when she felt the palpable wall of
ol coming from Damien's end of the railing.

His face turned red with rage. Disappointment. Shock. 'No
onder you're hiding me out the back of the house where I
n't infect your family with my pestilence. Why did you even
other to go out with me at all if I am just one more example
the kind of filth you wouldn't deign to scrape off your shoe?'

A ray of sunlight suddenly shone from beneath a cloud
inging with it clarity, and renewed optimism. Or at least that
as how Chelsea felt.

His words were harsh. The harshest she'd ever heard him
ter. But hearing the hurt in his voice only made her realise
at he cared more than he'd ever let on.

And to find out just how much he really did care, she was
ing to have to give up a part of herself without any kind of
irety she would ever get it back. She was going to have to
amble more than she could afford to lose.

'Damien, I need you to really hear me. Okay?'

He didn't nod, but at least he didn't turn his back.

'This has all happened so quickly between us. I feel like I'v
been swept well and truly off my feet. And that could neve
have happened with someone I didn't trust. Someone I didn
truly believe was different from all the other guys who mad
me doubt your gender was worth the effort. Why is this s
hard?'

She ran a hand over her eyes, trying to subdue the risin
panic that it was already too late. And then she found dee
within herself a way to make him understand. She lifted he
eyes from the relative safety of the ground to his haunting eye
as she said, 'I've always thought that if people were only force
to wear T-shirts with signs on them the world would be a bette
place. Signs that said who they really were.'

A muscle continued to flicker in his jaw, but his teeth seeme
to unclench. The hard line of his mouth softened. He was a
least listening.

'Signs like Verbal Abuser with Mother Issues. Sel
Obsessive Narcissist. Sweet as Honey All the Way to the Bon
Shark in Goldfish Skin.'

She shook her hair off her face again before asking, 'I'd lov
to know what your T-shirt would say.'

He blinked slowly. 'I think it's more important right now fo
you to tell me what *you* think my T-shirt would say.'

The first word that came to mind was *Dreamy.* From the be
ginning he'd been a six-foot-something, broad-shouldered, de
licious dream of a man. But had he, at some stage over the pas
week, while she had been fluttering and floundering, an
finding reasons to keep him at arm's length, actually becom
real? Was he right alongside her struggling with the enormit
of what had *actually* happened between them?

She felt like a butterfly under a magnifying glass as h

erced her with his unrelenting gaze. And her mouth was so
y she couldn't hope to speak.

'Or do you want to know what I think your T-shirt should
y?' he asked.

Yes, she thought. *Desperately. But no. Not while you're
oking at me like that. All wounded and gorgeous. Not while
ur worlds are balancing on a knife's edge.*

She flapped a hand between them as though it didn't matter.
e caught it and pulled it to his chest and she stumbled after it
ntil she was bodily against him. Again. Exactly the same way
s they had been when they first met. At his nearness, her breath
hooshed from her lungs and a pulse began to beat erratically
her throat.

Only this time he wasn't a beautiful stranger; this time he
as a man with whom she had shared far more of herself, of
er thoughts, her dreams, her past, her body, and her innermost
lf than she had with any man.

She tried to pull away, but he only tugged her back, sliding
ne hand around her waist, stopping where the small of her
ack met the top of her jeans, pressing her against the full
ngth of him while with the other hand he turned her hand in
is until he held it over his heart. She could feel the pulse beat
rong and fast behind his ribs. And hers soon altered to match
is beat for beat.

A shriek of laughter spilled from somewhere inside the
ottage. A crash of saucepans was followed by Kensey's raised
oice scolding someone. But after about ten words the admon-
hment turned to laughter too.

'Come on,' Damien said. He held her hand and drew her
own the rambling, weed-encrusted back steps to the messy
ard below. Feeling like an emotionally overwrought rag doll,
he gave in and let him lead her where he may.

When they reached the shade of an old oak tree, Damien edged her around the side so that they were shielded from prying eyes by the shade of the large trunk and a curtain of drooping branches that almost touched the ground.

She leaned back against the tree, the bark digging into her back in twenty different places. He leant a hand beside her head, so close all she'd have to do was look left and she could nuzzle against his warm skin.

'I hurt you, didn't I? Trying to squeeze you to fit you into a compartment in my life like I do my job, my friends, my family?'

Okay, now this was getting really real. There was no artifice between them. No flirtation. No mobile phones to keep them at a comfortable distance.

'I'll live,' she said.

'I know you will. And I know I will too. But what I don't see is why either of us should just live. I want more than that. And I know you do too. I think… I believe that we owe it to ourselves to see if we might just be able to do it together. What can I do to make you trust me again?'

She shrugged. Tempted by the almost promise behind his words, but completely unsure it would be possible for her to trust anyone again, least of all herself.

'Your father really did a number on you, didn't he?'

She blinked up at him, sideswiped by the change of tack. 'Excuse me?'

'I'm not like him. Or the people who let him down. I'm here,' he said, 'even after you brushed me off. And I can tell you that took some kind of leap of faith on my part. Now it's your turn. Chelsea. Tell me about your father. What did he do to make you so unwilling to take a chance on us?'

The thread of apprehension for ever wrapped around

Chelsea's heart tightened, strangling her ability to do as he asked. But the thought of feeling that way, trapped between her desires and her fears for ever, suddenly felt too much. And just not fair.

She breathed in as deeply as she could until she felt the thread snap and her breath shuddered as it released. And she watched the pulse beating in the base of his neck as she said, 'He used to use us in his scams.'

Damien swore beneath his breath. 'Were you ever in any danger?'

'Not in the line of fire as far as I can remember. He was smart enough to move us onto a new place whenever he got close.'

'And when your family stayed out this way with the guy who could cook? The man with the dog?'

'I never knew how they knew one another. But I've always wondered if he was my uncle. My mum's brother. Whoever he was he made us go to school, and kept Dad on the straight and narrow for a full six months before we upped and moved in the middle of the night.'

'And your uncle loved dogs.'

'With all his heart.'

The questions dried up. She wondered if he'd found out what he wanted to know. If he had enough information to slap himself over the back of his head and tell himself to give up on her for good. The backs of her eyes burnt anew as she began to feel the pain that losing him now would cause.

'So you could really steal my wallet easy as you please,' he said. 'No joke.'

A shift in his voice made her look up. There was a glimmer in his eye. The tiniest glimmer, but enough that she knew that he was turned on. By her ability to hoodwink him. Hope sprang through her veins like the elixir of life.

'I might have done it a half dozen times already, and put it back, and you'd never have known.'

He leaned in towards her. If he kissed her now she wouldn't be able to stop him. But at the last second he pulled back. The hand beside her head moved to hover at her cheek, then clenched and tucked into the pocket of his trousers.

He looked past her into the distance. 'I don't chase women, Chelsea. Maybe because I've never had to. It may seem arrogant but it's the truth. I've never begged a woman to be with me. Then when I drove away, believing I might never see you again…' His eyes blazed and when he looked at her it was as if now he wasn't sure whether to kiss her senseless or wring her neck.

But the very fact that he was struggling at all meant the world. It meant her hope, her trust, had never been misplaced. Her instincts were right. He was different. He was worth the fight. And her spirit was not completely downtrodden yet.

'Damien…' she said, reaching out and laying a hand upon his chest. The moment her fingers curled into his cotton shirt his eyes darkened, his breaths grew deeper beneath her hand, and she knew she wasn't ready for him to not be there. Would never be. 'If you'd like to stay that would be okay with me.'

He breathed deep through his nose. All neck-wringing thoughts seemed to have dried up as his gaze dropped to her mouth. 'Never has a man heard happier words.'

'I meant for dinner,' she explained.

His gaze travelled up her warming cheek and back to her eyes. 'Are you sure?'

Sure? Sure that she wanted him back, even though he'd not once told her he loved her, or could promise her more than he already had? She'd never been less sure in her life. But she was willing to take the chance that he cared enough he might yet one day grow to love her.

She swallowed the lump in her throat. This was it. Time to
est her newly unfettered heart. 'I'm highly protective of my
amily. I've never invited a man to eat dinner with them before.'

His left eyebrow rose. 'Yet you chose me. A fully fledged
uit-and-tie conman?'

She nodded. 'And if you don't behave there are plenty of
places out here in which to hide a dead body.'

And for the first time since he'd arrived, he laughed. The
peautiful sound raced through her veins.

'That's my girl,' Damien said, leaning in against her flat-
ened hand until her elbow brushed against the tree and their
noses were mere inches apart.

'Will you stay?' she asked.

'I did come all this way,' he murmured.

'Stalker,' she said, biting back a smile.

'Cynic,' he shot back before closing the gap between them
and kissing her with such heat she clenched a fist into his shirt.

His tongue swooped into her mouth and took her breath
away with such intensity she truly believed he'd wanted to kiss
ner from the second he got out of the car.

He pulled back and whispered against her swollen lips, 'I
knew I missed you for a good reason.'

'If that's the only reason, then I warn you I consider that
already misbehaving.'

'If I get my way we'll both be misbehaving a hell of a lot
more before this night is done.' He leaned in and kissed her
again, with even less restraint than he had before.

And she let herself do the same. She let go. Completely.
Allowing her love for him to overflow, to tell him just how
much she missed him through *her* actions rather than her words.

He pulled away far too soon. 'I can smell dinner.'

'She's a bad cook. It can wait.'

He smiled. 'The sooner we eat, the sooner we can think about moving onto after-dinner pursuits.' He let her go, easily as you please, and walked past her headed back to the house.

She hugged her arms about herself, amazed anew that he had come. That he was staying. And that she was letting him. But the absolute truth was he wasn't the same man she'd left the night before. There was still something different about him. Some kind of calm resolution she couldn't put her finger on.

She wasn't sure if it was a good or bad thing, just that somehow, after today, things were never going to be the same again.

Her heart ached to know if this weekend would be a bitter-sweet end to the greatest week of her life. If he might stay with her a month. Two. Or if the whole dream really was there for the taking.

He turned to walk backwards, away from her. 'Coming?'

She pushed away from the tree and followed.

'Still want to know what I'd write on your T-shirt?' he asked as she approached.

She nodded.

'You'd need enough cotton to go to the moon and back to fit upon it all the things I think make you you.'

And with that he jogged up the weedy back steps and into the house.

CHAPTER THIRTEEN

CHELSEA followed Damien into the cottage on shaky legs to find the place in uproar. Kensey stood over Slimer with a tipped-over cake-mix pan while Slimer sat on his rug trying to lick the delicious mixed ingredients off his fur.

'Chelsea, thank God,' Kensey said. 'Can you do the honours while I whip up another batch? Lucy, stop crying, honey. There will be birthday cake.'

Chelsea kept on walking into the laundry where she found the Slimer pack: a bucket, soap, a pair of clippers, and a hard bristled brush.

'Slimer, outside,' she called out and turned to run smack bang into a hard wall of Damien.

'I'll give you a hand.'

She glanced at his beautiful suit with the paw-print stains already baked on. Then thought that if she left him inside how quickly the kids would smell fresh blood and climb all over him and what else Kensey would let on if she wasn't there to stop her.

'Are you sure? It's getting cold out and I can do it by myself.'

'Not gonna happen,' he said, shucking off his jacket and laying it casually atop the dryer.

Her certainty there had been some kind of change in him intensified until it actually gave her goose-bumps. 'I class being bossy as misbehaving.'

'Well, that's just tough. The way I see it I'm going to need a firm hand if we are going to have any kind of chance at turning this crazy attraction into what it seems determined to become. So get over yourself and let me be there for you.'

He reached out and took a hold of the handle of the bucket, his thumb brushing against hers, sending sparks of electricity from her hand to his.

'What this seems determined to become?' she repeated, fixated on the words rather than the dark, dangerous look in his eye.

His voice dropped as he said, 'I have no intention of having *that* conversation in a place that smells like wet dog and detergent.'

She wasn't letting him off the hook that easy. 'If you want anything to do with me, Slick, you're going to have to get used to the smell.'

He rolled his eyes to the heavens. 'Hell, Chelsea, I wouldn't want to do it surrounded by computer terminals and screaming, overworked day traders either.'

It? What it?

'Fine,' she said, letting go and sliding past him, through the kitchen and outside to the grassy area at the side of the cottage. 'Slimer! Here!'

Slimer came bounding outside, as usual too thick to realise what the hose in her hand meant until she had him chained to the clothesline.

Damien followed in his wake, dark and broad and beautiful in his designer threads with muddy dog prints on his chest, dead leaves attached to the bottoms of his shoes, and a crazed old bucket in his hand. He still looked out of place, but beautifully so.

She turned on the hose and he kept on coming. Let him get his perfect clothes all wet and muddy. Then he'd really see how literally messy her life was.

'Come here, boy,' she called out. Slimer came to her, she held out the hose and at the last second he darted away. She instinctively tipped the hose in the opposite direction to herd him back where she wanted him.

The shout that came from Damien's direction swung her gaze his way to find him standing with his feet shoulder-width apart, his face dripping with water, a neat spray covering his shirt and the bottom of his trousers soaked. He looked so shocked, she had to bite her lips to stop from laughing.

He looked up at her, his eyes blazing. 'You did that on purpose.'

'Did not.'

He took a gigantic step towards her and she squealed. She held the hose in front of herself as a shield.

He shook the droplets from his hair which left it spiky and left him looking like something out of a magazine photo spread. With his dark eyes, stormy expression and clothes clinging wetly to him he was unbelievably hot.

'Don't you dare tell me you're turned on right now,' he demanded, and her eyes shot from the fabric stretching across his thighs to his face and her cheeks turned a degree warmer.

But *his* eyes were now dancing. Bright and beautiful and laughing.

She cocked her hip and let the water tilt away from him. 'And what if I am? Watcha gonna do about it?'

He took another step her way and she baulked. The hint of a smile quickly turned into a devilish grin. Then he moved with such speed she brought the hose between them only to have his hand clasp down on hers. The water shot skyward, showering them both in a thick spray of water.

Slimer barked and frolicked and generally loved the fact that anyone else was getting wet bar him.

Chelsea screamed, and tried to kick Damien in the shin but he was too quick. He turned the hose on her full blast, her hair flew back from her face and her white long-sleeved T-shirt soon became sodden.

When the water spray disappeared, she spat out a clump of hair and opened her eyes to find Damien standing before her staring hard at her breasts. She looked down to find her T-shirt and beige bra had become completely see-through. Her cold nipples stood out hard and dark through the thin fabric.

He dragged his gaze to her face, and her breath caught in her lungs at the level of desire surging behind his eyes.

Love me, she thought with such desperation he must have heard. Instead she said, 'Don't even think about it. There are kids just inside the house.'

'I know,' he said, his voice a deep growl. 'But if there weren't, I want you to know that your dry-cleaner would be trying to get grass stains from your clothes come Monday.'

'I don't have a dry-cleaner. Like most regular people I wash my own clothes.'

His mouth tilted into a smile. 'You're frozen solid, drenched to the bone, without a weapon, and breathing so hard you look like you are about to pass out from it, yet you still manage to dredge up a way to keep me from getting too big for my boots. I love you.'

His words hung on the air like snowflakes. Delicate, ethereal and in danger of melting away lest she pay close attention. Chelsea licked her suddenly dry lips. 'Did you just say—'

'I did,' Damien said, his own breaths suddenly coming harder. He reached over and turned off the hose at the tap and the world turned silent. Even Slimer chose that moment to have a little lie-down.

Damien let the hose slump at his feet and walked over to where Chelsea stood shivering, much less from the cold than from the events consuming her.

He reached out and ran his hands up and down her arms, warming her, inside and out. And then he closed the gap completely and drew her to him and kissed her. Softly, fully, deeply and full of the feelings he had just admitted.

When he pulled away and looked down into her eyes Chelsea wasn't shaking any more. She wasn't scared, she wasn't unsure, she wasn't even the least bit overwhelmed. She loved him and he...he was real, after all.

'Since I drove away from you last night,' he said, his voice low and intimate and true, 'I have been miserable. Wretched even. But hitting that low was what I needed to realise that you are my high. I drove here planning on whisking you away somewhere beautiful, and most of all somewhere private in order to convince you of what I feel for you.'

'Here's fine,' she said, her voice breathless.

He smiled, crinkles fanning out from the edges of his stunning eyes. 'So it is. Now for this moment to at least end the way I planned for it to end I need you to look me in the eye and know, to the bottom of your heart, that I have gone right ahead and fallen madly in love with you.'

Chelsea did as she was told. She looked into his Pacific-blue eyes, and saw the truth. The whole truth. That was the difference she saw in him. He not only loved her, but he was ready to love her and to keep on loving her.

'I'm in love with you too,' she blurted, the words spilling from her like a rainbow splashed across a rain-cleansed sky. 'From the moment I met you you made me feel like for the first time in my life I could dream as big as I wished. You may own a suit or two, and you may be a touch arrogant, but that's only scratching the surface. You're good and kind and generous and fun and playful and you're hot. Have I even told you how beautiful I think you are? And tall. I lo-o-ove that you're really tall. And when you kiss me…'

Her next words were lost within the warmth of his lips. *Thank God,* she thought, because once she'd opened the flood gates she felt as if she could go on and on for ever telling him how alive he made her feel.

He slid the wet cotton of her T-shirt upwards until his warm hand made direct contact with her waist and before she knew it his thumbs were running along the undersides of her breasts.

'Hey, guys, is Slimer done?' Kensey came round the side of the house and Chelsea hid behind Damien and tugged her shirt back into place.

Kensey placed a hand on her hip and glared at them, though Chelsea caught the delighted twinkle in her eye. 'My dog is now covered in cake mix *and* is muddy and wet. And you lot look just as bad. Can I not leave any of you alone for just one second?'

'We'll wash him now,' Damien said. 'I promise.'

'Mmm. You'd better. Though if you turn out to be a bad influence on my little sister, Damien Halliburton, I may just kiss you myself.' Kensey winked, turned tail and left.

'She means it,' Chelsea warned.

'I don't doubt it.'

Damien grabbed the hose, Chelsea the brush and they had Slimer clean in five minutes flat. She rubbed him down with a towel and sent him running in the direction of the house.

'I'm getting the feeling,' he said, wiping his hands down the only dry patches of his trousers, 'the events of this past week, the loss of my phone, the stalker claims, the animal-print-underwear fiasco, the food poisoning, aren't actually anything unusual for those in the London family. This is what life with you is really going to be like from now on, isn't it?'

When she looked back over her shoulder and realised just how wet Damien was, wet and still beautiful, while she must have looked like a drowned rat, Chelsea burst into laughter.

She padded up to him and threw herself into his arms, snuggling up to him, sliding her cold hands beneath his clothes and up his warm back. 'If I admit it is are you going to leave and never come back?'

He nibbled at the soft skin below her ear. 'No. I'm thinking I could get very used to your life. So much so, in fact, it would mean less nights on Caleb's couch and more at your apartment, I'm afraid.'

She shrugged, her breasts rubbing deliciously against his front. 'We've proven my bed's big enough for the two of us. And I loved how you looked in my kitchen. And my shower. And on my couch. I could get very used to that too. Move in with me.'

He looked down into her eyes, searching, hoping, dreaming as big as she'd ever seen any man dream as the idea of moving in with her obviously sat well on his shoulders.

A light sprinkle of autumn rain fluttered against her eyelids. She blinked them away and held her man tighter still. *Her man.* The man of her dreams. Whatever she'd done to deserve this, to deserve him, she was planning on doing it a whole lot more.

'It would be my pleasure,' he said. 'Though I do have some things in storage I'd like to bring over to make me feel more at home. A couch and some bookshelves and a desk and some appliances I'll need if we are going to eat anything more nutritious than leftovers.'

'I like leftovers,' she said as she nipped at his neck.

'I hate chintz,' he warned as he angled his chin to give her better access.

'I hate dark leather and stainless steel.'

'Of course you do. But I washed a dog today.'

'You did.'

'So next week you come to a bar with me.'

It wasn't a question. Chelsea sank further against him. 'I'll come. I'll even play tennis with your parents. But I won't drink Martinis. I prefer Harvey Wallbangers with my sporting endeavours.'

'You can play tennis?'

'Surprised?'

Damien grinned down at her as he slid his right thigh gently between hers. 'Infinitely.'

Chelsea's phone buzzed in her back pocket.

'Leave it,' he said.

'Can't. Might be important. Life-changing even.'

She flipped open to find a message from Kensey:

CHELSEA! DAMIEN! DINNER!

'We have to go in now or we'll be in big trouble,' she said, sliding her phone back away.

Damien growled as he disentangled himself from her. 'Will I never get past second base with you again?'

'Tonight,' she promised.

'So I'm staying after dinner now, am I?'

'If you don't mind sharing a room with me, which is on a different floor from the bathroom, has creaky floorboards and a lumpy double bed.'

'Well…'

'What if I guarantee you a home run? Or two if you're very nice to me.'

'That's the best you can offer?'

'Fine,' she said on a sigh. 'I can guarantee the same the next ay and the next. If that's what it will take to get you inside now efore Kensey blows her lid.'

'Minx,' he said, rubbing her nose with his.

'Hunka Hunka,' she said, kissing him hard, and long, and ow before ducking under his arm and running towards the ouse.

He caught her in about three steps, grabbed her around the aist and threw her over his shoulder. She kicked but soon dis-olved into raucous laughter. 'So this is what life with a alliburton is going to be like,' she managed to say between iggles.

'Sweetheart, you have no idea what you're in for.'

And while a week ago the thought of having no idea what e days ahead might bring would have frightened her silly, she et herself droop until she could slide her hands into the back ockets of his jeans and she hung on tight. And grinned. From ar to ear. Because she knew the most important thing—he'd e there with her.

Damien slapped her on the butt, shifted her into a more omfy position on his broad shoulder and carried her into the reat big beautiful future.

Silhouette®

SPECIAL EDITION™

FROM *NEW YORK TIMES* BESTSELLING AUTHOR

LINDA LAEL MILLER

A STONE CREEK CHRISTMAS

Veterinarian Olivia O'Ballivan finds the animals in Stone Creek playing Cupid between her and Tanner Quinn. Even Tanner's daughter, Sophie, is eager to play matchmaker. With everyone conspiring against them and the holiday season fast approaching, Tanner and Olivia may just get everything they want for Christmas after all!

Available December 2008
wherever books are sold.

Visit Silhouette Books at www.eHarlequin.com LLMNYTBPA

HARLEQUIN *Presents*

---

kept for his *Pleasure*

She's his mistress on demand

Whether seduction takes place in his king-size bed,
a five-star hotel, his office or beachside penthouse,
these fabulously wealthy, charismatic and sexy men
know how to keep a woman coming back for more!
Commitment might not be high on his agenda—or
even on it at all!

She's his mistress on demand—but when he wants her
body and soul, he will be demanding a whole lot more!
Dare we say it…even marriage!

Available in October
HOUSEKEEPER AT HIS BECK AND CALL
by **Susan Stephens**
#2769

Don't miss any books in this exciting new miniseries
from Presents!

Coming next month:
TAKEN BY THE BAD BOY
by Kelly Hunter #2778

www.eHarlequin.com

HPI2769

Wedlocked!

Legally wed,
But he's
never said,
"I love you."
They're…
Wedlocked!

**The series where marriages are made in haste…
and love comes later….**

Chef Lara needs cash—fast. Tall, dark, brooding
Wolfe Alexander needs to marry, and sees his opportunity.
He'll help Lara if she'll be his convenient wife….

Available in October

PURCHASED: HIS PERFECT WIFE

by **Helen Bianchin**

#2763

Look out for more WEDLOCKED! marriage stories
coming soon in Harlequin Presents.

www.eHarlequin.com

HP12763

REQUEST YOUR FREE BOOKS!

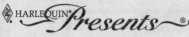 HARLEQUIN *Presents*®

2 FREE NOVELS PLUS 2 FREE GIFTS!

YES! Please send me 2 FREE Harlequin Presents® novels and my 2 FREE gifts (gifts are worth about $10). After receiving them, if I don't wish to receive any more books, I can return the shipping statement marked "cancel". If I don't cancel, I will receive 6 brand-new novels every month and be billed just $4.05 per book in the U.S. or $4.74 per book in Canada, plus 25¢ shipping and handling per book and applicable taxes, if any*. That's a savings of close to 15% off the cover price! I understand that accepting the 2 free books and gifts places me under no obligation to buy anything. I can always return a shipment and cancel at any time. Even if I never buy another book, the two free books and gifts are mine to keep forever.

106 HDN ERRW 306 HDN ERRL

Name   (PLEASE PRINT)

Address   Apt. #

City   State/Prov.   Zip/Postal Code

Signature (if under 18, a parent or guardian must sign)

Mail to the **Harlequin Reader Service:**
IN U.S.A.: P.O. Box 1867, Buffalo, NY 14240-1867
IN CANADA: P.O. Box 609, Fort Erie, Ontario L2A 5X3

Not valid to current subscribers of Harlequin Presents books.

Want to try two free books from another line?
Call 1-800-873-8635 or visit www.morefreebooks.com.

* Terms and prices subject to change without notice. N.Y. residents add applicable sales tax. Canadian residents will be charged applicable provincial taxes and GST. Offer not valid in Quebec. This offer is limited to one order per household. All orders subject to approval. Credit or debit balances in a customer's account(s) may be offset by any other outstanding balance owed by or to the customer. Please allow 4 to 6 weeks for delivery. Offer available while quantities last.

Your Privacy: Harlequin Books is committed to protecting your privacy. Our Privacy Policy is available online at www.eHarlequin.com or upon request from the Reader Service. From time to time we make our lists of customers available to reputable third parties who may have a product or service of interest to you. If you would prefer we not share your name and address, please check here. ☐

HP08R

Playboy princes, island brides—
bedded and wedded by royal command!

Roman and Nico Magnati—
Mediterranean princes with undisputed
playboy reputations!

These powerfully commanding princes expect their
every command to be instantly obeyed—and they're not
afraid to use their well-practiced seduction to get want
they want, when they want it....

Available in October

HIS MAJESTY'S MISTRESS
by *Robyn Donald*
#2768

Don't miss the second story in Robyn's brilliant duet,
available next month!:

THE MEDITERRANEAN PRINCE'S
CAPTIVE VIRGIN
#2776

www.eHarlequin.com   HP12768

BROUGHT TO YOU BY FANS OF HARLEQUIN PRESENTS.

We are its editors and authors
and biggest fans—and we'd
love to hear from YOU!

Subscribe today to our online blog at
www.iheartpresents.com

HPBLOG

HARLEQUIN *Presents* EXTRA

MEDITERRANEAN DOCTORS

Demanding, devoted and
drop-dead gorgeous—
These Latin doctors will
make your heart race!

Smolderingly sexy Mediterranean doctors

Saving lives by day…red-hot lovers by night

**Read these four Mediterranean Doctors stories
in this new collection by your favorite authors,
available in Presents EXTRA October 2008:**

THE SICILIAN DOCTOR'S MISTRESS
by SARAH MORGAN

THE ITALIAN COUNT'S BABY
by AMY ANDREWS

SPANISH DOCTOR, PREGNANT NURSE
by CAROL MARINELLI

THE SPANISH DOCTOR'S LOVE-CHILD
by KATE HARDY

www.eHarlequin.com   HPE1008